AQUA
erotica

AQUA
erotica

edited by
mary anne mohanraj

 *A Melcher Media DuraBook*

 Three Rivers Press NEW YORK

See page 208 for additional credits.

AQUA EROTICA copyright © 2000 by Melcher Media, Inc.

Published by Three Rivers Press, New York, New York.
Member of the Crown Publishing Group.
Random House, Inc.
New York, Toronto, London, Sydney, Auckland
www.randomhouse.com

Three Rivers Press is a registered trademark and the
Three Rivers Press colophon is a trademark of Random
House, Inc.

DuraBooks™, patent pending, is a trademark of
Melcher Media, Inc. The DuraBooks™ format utilizes
revolutionary technology and is completely waterproof
and highly durable.

Printed in China.

Library of Congress Cataloging-in-Publication Data is
available upon request.

ISBN 0-609-80656-4

10 9 8 7 6 5 4 3 2 1

First Edition

For Jedediah

Contents

by Mary Anne Mohanraj

When I was first asked to edit this anthology, it sounded like great fun. Water is so obviously a natural subject for erotica. Water is inherently sexy: it can be gentle, warm, delicious.

I expected the collection to be full of light stories, delightful little erotic tales—cheerful, like a bubbling spring. There are certainly more than a few of those in this book. Diane Kepler's "Hydrodynamica" is a tale of a student who is having a very difficult time studying her fluid dynamics; Kris Hawes gives us a teasing woman and her partner (who must choose between basketball and a steamy shower) in "Velvet Glove," and Thomas Roche's poor artist's model writhes delightfully on her couch in "Watercolor." These stories are rich, heartfelt, often complex; their playfulness is seductive and sexy. But not all the stories are so light-hearted.

There were dark currents in many of the stories I received. Love and lust, certainly—but also pain and betrayal, deaths by drowning. Some of the pieces were so painful that they moved me to tears as I read them. Bill Burkett's "Addiction" tells the story of a man trapped by his own desires, struggling to escape them; "Movements," by Michael Hemmingson, chronicles what may be the end, or new beginning, of a marriage, and the lengths to which a man will go to save it. A few stories pushed even further—Simon Sheppard's "In Deep" explores the boundaries of consent, loss of control, and the desire for sexual oblivion; it terrified me even as it fascinated.

At first, I was concerned about including too many stories that probed beyond the rosy surface of sex into murky territory; I agonized about the overall feel of the book, and wondered whether I needed to search harder for more "positive" depictions of sexuality.

Perhaps I'd been conditioned by reading so much "sex-positive" erotica. Those of us writing and editing in this field have spent years struggling to reclaim erotic writing from the realm of the dank adult bookstore, the brown paper wrapper, the surreptitious reading in the dark—where your parents/wife/husband/kids won't catch you. In those days, many of us wrote cheerful, fun little stories, skimming along the surface of pleasant (and societally approved) desires. Simple stories were safer. Back in the days when finding an erotic novel in a mainstream bookstore was startling, writing or editing an erotic book with dangerous currents would have been taking a huge risk.

But these days, we no longer have that excuse. The climate of the country is changing, and now every major bookstore seems to have its erotica shelf or shelves—sometimes you'll even find erotica right there with literature. Maybe the field has grown up a little; we're not dipping our toes into the pool anymore—we're diving in, exploring the deeper realms of desire. Scary things live in the depths—desires for sexual oblivion, pain, infidelity, betrayal, and pure lust—but we are facing them, embracing them.

In my own writing, I'm finding myself examining consensuality much of the time; I'm fascinated by what constitutes consent, by what happens when we push past (or ask, beg, to be pushed past) our own boundaries. I'm also interested by silence, by the desires that are left unspoken. So many of us have fears and hesitations about sexuality, yet at the same time have these painfully strong desires—I know from my own experience that there can be an incredible rush, a powerful sexual excitement, derived from crossing the boundaries of the forbidden. That rush can come from something as simple (and frightening) as opening your mouth and asking for what you really want.

This is undoubtedly difficult material; it's treacherous and takes careful handling. Some might argue that it's safer to leave these waters unexplored; none of us want to accidentally blur the line between fantasy and reality. But what is good for us is not always the same as what is safe, and I must believe that if there are monsters in these waters, that it is better to know their strengths and weaknesses, to understand fully the power they have over our bodies and souls.

Sexuality has a dark side, but we will never grow up if we close our eyes and pretend it isn't there. For decades authors have been examining the complexities of love and desire in some areas of sexuality, in the realm of the permissible; now we can openly take those discussions further. Read and explore and embrace these stories—let these authors lead you through your own explorations. Let them use water (sunlit and stormy) to delineate the shades and moods of desire. In the end, I am very pleased to have received so many powerful stories that respond to the elemental natures of water and of sex. I hope you find yourself responding similarly to their strength and beauty, allowing the water to carry you to the heart of your desires.

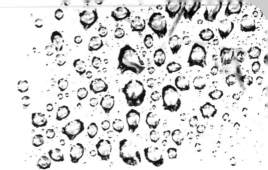

I Want

MARY MAXWELL

I WANT TO MAKE LOVE IN THE HEAT.

A desert road, straight and level, as relentless as desire. The broken yellow line runs beside the car—dash, dash, dash—like a Morse code message repeating endlessly. The distant hills are red-brown, worn as smooth as the curves of a woman's body. The land by the road is dusted with alkali, white as laundry detergent spilled from the box. We haven't seen another car for hours.

On the road ahead, a mirage shimmers—black water on the asphalt, reflecting the sky. As we drive toward it, the pool evaporates, disappearing without a trace. It's the heat, I know, that makes mirages. The air above the hot road bends the light, reflecting it back to show me what I want to see. Hot road; cool water. It's the heat that does it.

"Stop the car," I say.

"Why?" you ask.

"Just stop."

The road is smooth and hot beneath my bare feet. My shoes are in the car, jumbled with the maps, books, bits and pieces of travel detritus. Too hot. I take the water jug and spill some water on the pavement, on the yellow line that marks the blacktop.

"What are you doing?" you ask.

"Making a mirage," I say. Then I pull my tank top over my head. "And going for a swim." I pull off my shorts and stand naked on the wet asphalt.

You stay by the car, laughing.

"Come here," I say.

"Suppose someone comes by."

"Come here."

Still laughing, you come to me and I kiss you, dropping my hands to trace the curve of your shoulders, your back, your ass. "You're overdressed," I tell you. "It's too hot for this." I pull your T-shirt over your head, exposing your breasts to the sun. Your arms and neck are tanned, but your breasts are pale. I cup one in each hand, running my thumbs over the nipples, rubbing until they harden under my touch. You make a sound in your throat—a whimper of protest. We shouldn't be here; we shouldn't do this.

I kneel in the splash of water and take one nipple into my mouth, teasing it with my tongue until you moan. You taste of salt. I drop my hand from your breast, trailing it across your stomach. You are still wearing your shorts, but I reach up into the loose leg opening, stroking your inner thigh. Soft skin there, as pale as your breasts.

"Lie down," I tell you.

You're not laughing now. "Not here. In the car."

"Here."

"In the car."

I shake my head and lie back on the road, smiling. The asphalt is wet against my back. The heat of the road has already warmed the water. I can feel the smoothness of the yellow line, a little cooler than the black asphalt. The sun is dazzling. I squint up at your face against the sky. Blue sky, without a cloud.

You hesitate, then kneel beside me, placing your hand on my belly. "This is silly," you say, but I take your hand and move it across my breasts. "Suppose a truck comes along."

"There'll be no trucks," I say. I kiss your fingers one by one. My hand moves against the crotch of your shorts, rubbing you through the thin fabric. "Lie down."

Reluctantly, you lie beside me. I prop myself on one elbow to look down at you. You've closed your eyes against the sun, and you're breathing faster now. My hand moves against you. I can feel the fabric growing wet beneath my hand; I can smell you—sweet musky scent, forbidden perfume.

Beneath your head, the wet asphalt glistens in the sun. I slide my hand inside the elastic waistband of your shorts, inside the elastic of your panties. My fingers stroke the wet folds of your cunt—so welcoming, bringing moisture to the desert. You moan and lift your hips to push against my hand. Greedy, very greedy. I finger your clitoris, teasing it as I teased your nipple. You gasp, pushing harder against me.

The sun is hot on my back as I lean over and suck on your nipple. There's a trickle of sweat on your temple. I am sweating too, a trickle running down my breast. Water to the desert. I slip a finger inside you. You are warm and soft and wet and the desert smells of you, musky and strong. I slip another finger into your cunt, sweet cunt, hot as the desert. You are pushing against me now, pushing hard against my fingers.

I fuck you with my hand. Your eyes are closed; your breath catches in your throat as if you were sobbing, as if you had run too far, too fast, in the heat of the desert sun. My thumb finds your clitoris, wet and hard, a knot of flesh in the petals of a flower. You rock beneath me, insistent, demanding. It's the heat that does it— hot road beneath you; hot sky above.

When you come, you cry out and I feel your cunt clutching at my hand, gripping my fingers, holding me as if you will never let go. Greedy cunt—I like them greedy. Greedy and hot and wet.

I want to fuck you on a desert road to nowhere, by a pool of water that never was. I want to make love to you in the heat.

And you—where do you want to make love?

New House

DANIEL JAMES CABRILLO

THE HOUSE IS EMPTY, NEVER BEEN LIVED IN. CUSTOM-BUILT, NO expense spared, by an investment banker recently indicted for fraud and attacked by his heart. Dead at forty-four.

The real estate agent knows me by now, knows she's going to sell me something—if not this house at two million dollars, then another at two million dollars.

She unlocks the door for me. "Look around," she says. "Take pictures, take your time."

"When you go," she says, "just close the door and make sure it's locked."

I nod; the real estate agent leaves me alone.

I tend to be impulsive, but I know it, and so in this instance I'm being very careful. I want the house, my wife wants the house, we will probably buy the house, but we're slowing ourselves down, forcing ourselves to look around at what else is available.

I keep coming back here, though—two, three, four times.

The house is Spanish in style, two stories, with white walls and terra-cotta floors, U-shaped in layout and built around a cloistered garden. Each room affords vistas through arches into adjacent rooms and across the garden. It has never looked better than it does now, in the late afternoon sun. I'm already comfortable in it; it already feels as if it were mine. Photographing it, I feel the same familiarity with it that I feel when I take family pictures.

I step into the garden, cross to the open side, and turn back to take a picture of the house across the cloister.

A woman steps into the doorway just as the shutter snaps. She is as surprised to see me as I am to see her.

"Oh," she says. "Sorry."

"That's all right," I say. "Makes a better picture."

It does make a better picture: the woman is a pretty ash-blonde, willowy and tan; her summer yellow dress splashes bright against the white stucco and terra-cotta. She holds in her nervous hands a big-brimmed straw hat with a colorfully printed silk scarf rolled up and tied at the base of the crown.

"Are you looking for the agent?" I ask as I cross the garden to join her.

"Just saw the for-sale sign on the lawn and the door open," she says.

"Good. Look around," I say. "Maybe the competition will make me bid."

"I'm not competition," she says. "I'm just looking."

"Well, help yourself; it's not mine yet."

The woman nods and goes back inside the house. She has a long, athletic, purposeful stride. Sexy.

I take a few more pictures of the exterior, then reenter the house, stroll from room to room. Now and then I take a picture, but I guess I'm really looking for the woman.

I find her upstairs in the big, empty master suite, which extends the whole width of the house. I see her from the hall; she's standing at the window with her back to me, looking out at the view. I can't resist, and take her picture.

The sound of the shutter alerts her to my presence. She turns to face me.

"You don't mind, I hope," I say.

She shrugs, leans back on the windowsill and stretches her legs straight out, studies me for a moment, then pushes herself away from the window and enters the bathroom. I step into the bedroom and snap a few shots of her as she appears through the portal, investigating the huge marble bathroom.

"You're a terrific subject," I tell her when she rejoins me. I mean it but feel a little silly saying it. "I mean," I add, "you and that yellow dress in this empty house . . ."

She accepts that without comment and goes into the hallway, then down the stairs. I follow, remaining a room away, photographing her through the arched portals as she moves from room to room, exploring, touching surfaces, leaning, bending, turning. She's got a knack for modeling. As the sun sinks lower, she intuitively finds the light pouring through windows and steps into it, strikes poses that don't look like poses; her bearing is dancerlike, natural and spontaneous.

The sun sets and bathes the house in gold.

I reload my camera with fast film. When I'm done I have to search for her. I find her seated on the living room floor, her skirt pulled up across her thighs, her hands folded in her lap. I take a picture through an arch, then step into the room, cross to her, stand above her looking down.

I don't know where this is going. I am, I should explain to those who care about such things, a faithful husband—in practice, never in thought. I flirt too much and do like to test limits. So far I haven't crossed the line. But I've never said never.

Here is a test I might, if all goes well, fail.

She knows I'm there but doesn't look up right away; when finally she does, we lock eyes. I don't smile; neither does she at first, but then the almost tangible sexuality within the room embarrasses her, and she smiles, blushes, and looks down at her hands in her lap.

She knows I want her to be sexy for my camera, but she's too self-conscious.

"Put on the hat," I say, reading her mind.

"What?"

"The hat. Put it on."

She puts on the hat, drops her head. I can no longer see her face, and she can't see me, but that's okay, that's the point: with the hat to hide behind she can pose less self-consciously. It seems to work, but slowly. Anonymous under the hat, she gradually forgets my presence, though not the camera's; the rhythm of her movements and her poses are directly related to the sound of the shutter.

She puts her hands on the floor behind her, rests her weight on them, thrusts her bosom upward, extends her legs and crosses them at the ankle.

I take her picture.

She lies flat on her back, extends her arms straight out and spreads her legs, as if trying to fit inside one of Leonardo's circles.

I take her picture.

She turns onto her side and draws up fetal, her crossed arms between her legs.

I take the picture.

She unfolds, sits again, bends forward at the waist, her wrists still between her legs. She draws her hands upward, slowly running her fingertips along her lower belly.

Snap.

She stands up, runs her hands up her dress front, over her breasts to her neck, then takes the brim of the hat in both her hands, holds it as she twists away from me in one direction, then the other.

Every time I snap she changes her position; every time she changes her position I snap. It's hard to tell who's responding to whom.

Abruptly and without acknowledging me, she strides into the powder room and closes the door.

While she's in the powder room I check the film in my camera and look in my bag to see how much more I have. Three rolls of the very fast film I'll need in the fading light. I wish I had more but I'll make do.

The door to the powder room opens; the woman emerges and disappears into the next room, the dining room.

As I go after her, I glance into the powder room: the woman has left her bra, panties, and stockings behind, draped over the sink.

I continue on my way.

There is, it almost goes without saying, an excitement building in me, but it is an unfamiliar excitement—sexual, of course, but more than merely sexual—it is an excitement churning with curiosity and danger and guilt and charged by a magnetic energy that not only overcomes any trepidation I may have, but bullies it and mashes it into insignificance. There is no way, I know, for me to resist the impulses driving me.

From the dining room I can see into the room beyond, a den or family room; beyond that, through an open door, I can see outside to the swimming pool. The woman has gone around the pool and sits at its edge with her feet in the water, facing me. She's very far away, but she makes a pretty picture from where I am, and I take it.

I take another picture from the family room, then step outside, aim my camera again . . .

She unbuttons the buttons on her dress, first from the top down to the waist, then from the bottom up; when she's done only one button at her waist remains buttoned.

Slowly swishing her feet in the water, she slips one hand under the unbuttoned top of the dress and touches one of her breasts; she slides her other hand up between her legs and very gently strokes herself.

I step up to the edge of the pool, take a picture across it; the picture includes the woman and the reflection of the woman in the water.

I walk around the pool, stand beside her, looming over her, point my camera down and snap a picture from above—it's almost an abstract, dominated by the round hat brim and colorful scarf, her hands disappearing behind yellow fabric.

I crouch down; she tilts her head to make sure the brim still conceals her face; I take another picture, this one more clearly defining what her hands are doing.

I lower my camera, take a breath. I know what I'm going to do, and though it should surprise me, it doesn't, under the circumstances. I reach out and unbutton the one buttoned button on her dress.

The dress falls open, reveals her naked body—her breasts, smallish but plump and pretty, her gently rounded belly, her tuft of ash-blond pubic hair. As the dress opens she clamps her legs together and extends them straight out over the water, then places her hands over her breasts, fingers apart, letting the pink nipples show through.

I remain crouching and take more pictures.

She lies back—the hat brim falls over her face—and lifts her legs upward, squeezes her breasts, then releases them and slides her fingertips down her belly; when they reach her center she spreads her legs and drops her feet back into the water. With the fingers of one hand she separates her plump pussy lips and with the index and middle finger of the other hand turns little circles around her pink button.

I press the camera button but it doesn't snap; I'm out of film. Still crouching, I look dumbly at the camera, then at the woman's hands displaying her cunt and caressing her clit; I glide my glance upward over her stomach and tits to her shadowed face.

Her eyes peek out from under the hat brim; she's watching my eyes.

For the first time I am aware that I am in pain. My swollen cock is rock-hard but confined, squeezed flat against my belly by my trousers; the fabric creases my scrotum, squeezing and separating my balls.

I drop a knee to the ground, changing my crouch to a kneel, and feel better at once: the fabric imprisoning my cock loosens and gives freedom. My cock calls the shots now, pushing at the pants, pitching a tent.

I lay the camera aside and look at the woman's face again. As soon as I do she removes her hat and puts it on top of the camera.

Then she fixes her eyes on my crotch and resumes masturbating.

Her self-love stirs and inspires me; her steady gaze is my command. I unbuckle my belt and unzip my fly, and my pants fall to the ground at my knees; I push my shorts down too. I am totally focused on this woman. There is no muscle in me that does not ache with desire, no idea in my head that is not sexual; there is certainly no thought of possible consequences. I am all anticipation and expectation and greed. I want to attack, penetrate, envelop and be enveloped by her. And yet, though I am governed purely by lust, something inside me slows me down, tells me to take my time, hold back. I know that whatever happens with her will happen once and never again; the restraining impulse is my brain's way of telling my body not to blow it, to make the most of it.

When my cock bobs into view, stiff and a little shiny-sticky at the tip, the woman subtly alters the pace of her pussy-play: she slows the rotation of her fingertips but presses them harder against her clit.

Somewhere deep, deep down I know I have already crossed the line, and that there is probably no going back.

I rise to my feet and step out of the puddle of my pants and undershorts.

This is definitely wrong, but with a superhuman effort I might still save myself. Get dressed and get out of here . . .

I unbutton my shirt and pull it off. For a moment I'm not sure what to do next, what she wants me to do, what I want to do; so I simply stand in place, looking down at her, down past my own hard cock bobbing in my sight line, down to her hands in her pussy as she slips two fingers into her cunt, then slides them back out, her fingers flanking and caressing her clit in both directions. A moment later she arches her back and my attention is drawn to her puckered nipples atop her lovely tits, and then to her face, which expresses enthralled thoughts behind her closed eyes.

I don't know how I know it, but I know that I am not part of her thoughts, not really; and yet I know, too, that my presence is essential to her, is her catalyst; I know, finally, that we are living separate fantasies, that mine is her and hers is something I can't imagine.

She begins to heave herself up, arching her back so that only her shoulders and ass touch the concrete; her heels slap the pool water.

I step over her, straddle her, one foot on either side of her waist, my bobbing cock hovering over her navel and pointing up toward her face. She opens her eyes and looks at my cock head and the bead of moisture just forming there. I get down to my knees, kneeling. She sips a breath of air, holds it in her mouth. I put one hand on either side of her head and, on all fours, rock forward, aiming my cock at her face; she lifts her head and exhales, her breath a warm mini-breeze through my pubic hair and on my cock.

Suddenly, serpentlike, she darts her tongue forward and licks the moist bead from the tip of my cock. I am about to slide the shaft into her mouth when she tenses, tosses her head back, and cries out.

I straighten my back and look at her face for a moment. She's tensing, heaving, straining, beginning to come.

When she shuts her eyes, I put my hands on the cement on either side of her head and rest my weight on my extended arms. I hold myself over her and look back down under my torso to see her hips thrashing and bucking up to meet her hands in her cunt. And as I, on my hands and knees, watch her coming and listen to her choking, squealing, sighing, coming sounds, I am momentarily paralyzed; I know what I want but I know I can't have it. I want to penetrate and participate, to be with her when she comes. But how? I want my cock in her mouth. I want my cock in her cunt. I want to taste her sweet pussy. It isn't a matter of choosing which. I want it all.

She heaves herself up as she continues her climb; my cock strikes the top of her wrists. I look at her face, contorted with pleasure; she opens her eyes, winces briefly, looks into mine. She recloses her eyes, but she's not shutting me out, because at the same time she takes her hands out of her cunt, runs them up between our bodies, squeezes her tits, then quickly flings her arms around me, grabs on to my buttocks. I have to act now; she's not done coming and she expects me to finish for her.

I lower my head to her tits and suck—one, then the other—as I crawl backward along her length. She releases my buttocks, thinking I'm going to reposition myself to fuck her, but that's not what I do: I'm not ready yet. My feet, then my legs, enter the swimming pool—I tremble from the cold of the water but keep kissing her tits, then her stomach. I continue my slide into the pool, feet and legs first, then hips and cock—the cold water shocks my cock and retards my climb toward climax. When I am immersed to my chest, with my weight resting on my arms on the edge of the pool, I slide my hands under her buttocks, lift her hips, lower my face, and breathe on her cunt lips. As softly as I can, with just the barest contact, I tickle her clit with the tip of my tongue. At the moment of contact she jerks as if stunned by an electrical charge; she writhes; I try to keep caressing, my tongue tip following her clit as her ass dances in my hands, this way and that, this way and that.

I feast, in part tasting, in part testing, wanting to please her, trying to find what pleases her. I flatten my tongue, separate her pussy lips, press my tongue inward; she tastes the way I hoped she would—sweet and salty. Before long, however, she reaches down and, with her fingers, holds her lips open, exposing her clit to me, her way of letting me know that she prefers the gentle clitoral tongues to this lapping. I resume my tongue-flicking, from time to time sucking the button between my lips while licking its end with my tongue. Again she begins to thrash, bouncing her ass cheeks in my hands, turning her head from side to side, and when she resumes her climactic climb she removes her hands from her cunt and takes hold of my head, lifts, telling me that she wants me up.

I slide back up out of the pool, dripping over her as I move upward into position, on my knees between her outstretched legs. I lower my hips; the dome of my cock bobs, seeks, finds, nestles in her nook. I push. For a moment her matted hair bars the way, but not for long: she's so wet and I'm so hard that we won't be denied. After a brief tug, I enter . . . slide . . . in . . . in . . . in . . . into the slippery-wet warmth of her magic tunnel until my hairs mesh with hers . . .

And as soon as I am all the way in she heaves her hips up, presses her pelvis hard against mine, then drops her hips back to begin fucking, but I press downward against her and hold myself pressed there, motionless, resisting her upward thrusting. Almost desperately I want to slide my cock in and out of this fabulous warm tunnel, but I don't because I know that I'll come with the first thrust, and then it will be over. I don't want it to be over, and so I hold still. The woman wants to buck, to thrash, to squirm and fuck, but I won't have it; I remain glued against her, all my weight pressing down against her. She's reaching the climax of her climax now, though, and her spasms have to spasm someplace, so with her body thus imprisoned, she turns her spasms inward: I can feel them in the walls of her hot cunt surrounding my fully implanted shaft. Her muscle spasms feel like gripping goo, embracing my cock, enveloping it, squeezing it. The impulse to slide, to fuck actively, is almost irresistible, but I fight it; I hold myself buried but immobile until, at last, with her fingers gripping my ass, she flings her heels up out of the water and down onto the backs of my thighs, spasms, spasms again, and again, then deflates beneath me, spent.

We lie quietly for a while, my cock still hard and implanted, until her pulse slows and her breathing returns to normal. Then she pushes gently at my shoulders; I lift off of her, sliding my cock out slowly. When it emerges it makes an audible pop and the woman trembles. She gets to her knees, rolls me over onto my back, and leaves me there, flat on my back with my calves and feet in the water and my cock pointing straight up at the stars while she dives into the water.

She swims a few laps, and as she does I'm afraid her post-orgasmic calm will mean the end of the encounter—and I'm not finished. I needn't worry, though. Presently she gets out of the pool, dripping wet of course, crosses to me, kneels beside me. I look at her face and smile. She smiles too—a nice smile, sincere and even affectionate, but also a little sad. I reach out to touch the side of her face. As soon as I do, she leans down, drips water on my belly, takes my cock in her hand, lowers her face, enfolds the head of my cock between her lips, then draws the whole shaft inward, inward, swirling her tongue around as it slides deeper. I keep my eyes open throughout, for this woman understands the aesthetic as well as the tactile aspects of cocksucking. She sucks, she releases; when my cock emerges from her mouth, she holds it against her cheek and whirls her tongue around it. She lowers her breasts to it, kisses its tip with one nipple, then the other. She sucks it some more, releases it, holds it straight up in her hand, licks down to the balls, licks my balls, wetting them with pool water from her dripping wet hair and saliva, gently squeezes the wet balls in her hand as she runs her tongue tip up the ridge of the cock to the head, around the head rim, sucks in the whole head, the whole cock. She makes love to the cock, and the cock loves it, and she makes it last—skillfully altering her rhythms, now sucking, now licking, now merely caressing until, alas, it starts to dance the jerky dance of imminent climax. When the woman feels this, she stops sucking, holds the cock straight up, watches closely as a bead of white liquid appears at the tip, runs slowly down the head. She holds my cock at the root, squeezes to prevent further eruption, but she never takes her eye from the down-rolling drop of thick liquid. When it reaches the rim of my cock head, she takes the white droplet onto the tip of her pointed tongue and shows it to me. Then, still holding my cock straight up, quick as a flash she flings a leg over me, straddles me, and lowers her cunt onto my cock. She drops down, down, and when she's got me fully inside, she lifts, then plunges, lifts, then plunges, making sure that this time we fuck in earnest. And we do. I put my arms around her, pull her down flat against me, grip her ass and pull her down as I thrust up; then I hold tightly as I roll her over, turn her onto her back beneath me. As we turn my cock pops free but she grabs hold and pushes it back into her cunt. I lift her legs up, her feet on my shoulders, and plunge deep, but there's no stalling now; with the very first plunge my cock continues the process started in her mouth; it shoots . . . and shoots . . . and keeps shooting with each spastic plunge. I am growling like an animal, and she, too, is crying out with unexpected pleasure—unexpected because it comes so soon after her prior climax. When I feel I have little left, I release her legs; she drops them down; I flop between them and she wraps them around my legs as I fall on top of her and lie still, then jerk and jerk again with a series of frantic little aftershocks that keep this precious coupling alive and exciting until, finally, I collapse, utterly spent.

When we recover we start to dress. She simply slips into her dress and doesn't bother with her undergarments, so she's dressed first. I start to say something, but she puts her fingertip on my lips to hush me. Fair enough. Then she takes her finger away, kisses me there, and goes into the house.

By the time I get my shoes on and follow, she's gone.

I buy the house.

When my wife and I move in, the real estate agent gives us a portfolio of papers pertaining to the sale and to the house: the usual thing, inspection certificates, loan documents, et cetera. Also in the folder are tear sheets from a Sunday supplement article about the late, disgraced investment banker who had built the house. My wife reads the article and frowns.

"I feel sorry for the wife," says my wife.

"What?"

"Well, it was her house; you can tell by the picture."

I take a look. The picture shows the banker with his wife on the steps inside the house when it was still under construction. The banker strikes an arms-folded, nondescript camera pose, but his wife rests one arm on the banister railing. Her smile is obviously sincere, and the way she touches the railing is almost a caress.

"What an asshole," my wife says. "He builds her the house, doesn't even insure it, and dies. She gets nothing."

The woman in the picture wears a yellow dress, and in her hands she holds a wide-brimmed hat with a colorful scarf for a hatband.

Funny, I recognize the dress and hat first, then the face.

Hydrodynamica

DIANE KEPLER

PANIC IS SETTING IN.

I've got everything the experts recommend: a quiet room, a good reading lamp, a comfy chair, and more pencils than I could use in a year. But it's late, the exam is tomorrow, and I'm not prepared—even after spending all day at this desk.

And now, four chapters early, my brain is announcing that it's full.

The studying is taking its toll elsewhere, too. My eyelids, for example, feel as if they're edged with Velcro. Whenever they close, I have to rrrrrip them apart again. Eye muscles are delicate little things. I hate putting them through the Velcro ordeal, especially when they've spent the day dutifully scooting my eyes back and forth across pages of minuscule text.

Lids still closed, I lean forward. I press my face into an open book, taking in the scent of its white sheets and hoping a few equations will slip in through my pores. Fluid dynamics. Centuries of skull-sweat in a volume that weighs about as much as a small turkey. It's a miracle, really—everything I'd ever want to know for a mere

$79.95. But right now, I don't want to know. I want to sleep. Wait—first a roll in the hay with an intelligent, sensitive guy who doesn't back off when he finds out I'm majoring in physics. Then sleep.

Then an exam that I'm not prepared for.

I mutter a nasty word and raise my head once more.

In front of me there's a graph of something called the Dirac delta function. The diagram is completely flat, except at one place where it points excitedly at the ceiling. I can't help but think of it as Dirac's dick. Not that the rod of said physicist is in any way familiar. It's just impossible to look at that mathematical obscenity without comparing it to a schlong.

I smile at the carnal thought, but then push it aside.

Okay, Chapter 10. Bernoulli's principle.

In vector form, the equation is almost Modern in its simplicity and elegance. The inverted triangle in the center is called "del." God, what was Bernoulli thinking when he used that notation? Could it've been anything except the enticing triangle of fur atop his lover's pubic mound? Of course, that had to be it. No doubt the old goat was horny as hell when he'd written those famous formulas.

Then I catch on to what's happening. "Hey, no more smutty thoughts," I scold my unruly brain. "You'd better think about physics if you want any sleep."

But when I turn the page, I get a big shock, because right there in front of me is a portrait of Daniel Bernoulli, not as some crotchety old man with bad hair but as a vibrant youth. There's no telling if he really looked like that, but in this painting, the man is an absolute fox, reminding me of nothing so much as that guy from *Dangerous Liaisons*. He's got those same dark eyes and that same devilish profile. His brocade jacket and lace-fronted shirt look great. And instead of wearing the serious expression you see in nearly every eighteenth-century portrait, he looks as if he's stifling a mischievous grin.

I gaze at his picture while half-consciously pressing a hand to my crotch. Even through my jeans I can feel the warmth. Am I reacting this way because the book calls him one of the greatest scientists of the eighteenth century and I have a weakness for brainy guys? Or is it just because I haven't had any in months?

Ohh-kay. Time for a study break.

I slouch down in my chair and tilt the desk lamp so the light is out of my eyes. Then I imagine meeting him at—where did the bio say he worked? Russia. St. Petersburg in 1727, when Catherine I sat on the throne and fashionable women wore a half-dozen petticoats or more.

I'd meet him at some function. Maybe dinner at the house of a mutual friend. Or hell, why not go for grandeur? We meet at a ball. He's over on the other side of the room with a group of older men, and I'm flirting like mad from behind my fan because being laced into a corset—not really tight, that wasn't the fashion in those days—has always put me in the mood for some. No, no, can't say that. What can I say? Made me desirous of sexual congress? Yikes. How about made me dewy? Yes. "Her nether lips were bedewed with the juices of need." Mmm, oh yeah.

He notices my smoldering looks, a bit direct for a lady of quality, but that intrigues him and pretty soon he's bending over my hand. Not kissing it, because that's a bit much, but taking it in a grip that's gentle yet firm. It's as if he'd like to draw me toward him. A glance at his eyes confirms this. He's looking right at me with a gaze that's sharp and hot. I feel a shiver running up from between my legs. How interesting. I've known this man for two minutes and already my cranny is lubed up and aching for his touch.

Back in the twentieth century I undo my jeans and slide a hand past my own bushy del into a place that's gotten so slick I have to work to get a suitable amount of friction.

And in my mind, Daniel chats with me. I quiz him about his work on fluids. He seems delighted that I'm not a vapid cow and gives detailed replies even as he casts sidelong glances at my décolletage.

Then we dance. It's one of those scandalous new numbers from Paris and he presses me close. Even through my full complement of petticoats, I can tell there's something not entirely decent going on beneath his breeches. We drift off to the side of the jeweled ballroom where the autumn rain is beating against the windows and running down the leaded glass in intricate patterns.

"Just like inside you," he whispers.

I turn to him, somewhat taken aback. "I'm sorry?"

There's a naughty gleam in his eye. "Don't tell me you can't see the similarity."

I feel a rosy tint bloom on my cheeks. "Between the rain and—"

"Your most precious essence."

On the pane, with his fingers, he traces the paths made by the flowing water: a score of tiny rivulets that merge and divide. The pattern is repeated in veins on the inside of my wrist and these, too, he follows. When he paints me with lines of cool moisture, I understand the second meaning of his words. Still, the first remains uppermost in my mind, so I continue to ask him about his work. With a mischievous grin, he asks whether a tour of his lab would satisfy my curiosity. With a delicate arch of my brows, I confess that the sight of his apparatus would be most gratifying.

It's late, but in my fantasies there's always a carriage waiting. A cab pulls up and we cuddle together in its shadowy depths. The rain and the steady clip-clop of the horse's hooves drift in from beyond the velvet curtains, but they are nothing next to the sound of my heart as Daniel's moist lips make their way along my shoulder. He starts there and works his way up my throat, along my jaw, and then to my lips, which open wide in welcome. He claims my mouth by degrees. At first he is almost chaste. Next he is delicate, and then tender. But soon he is taking evident pleasure in nipping at the fullness of my lower lip and coaxing moans of pleasure from me with his agile tongue.

When my hand steals into his lap and strokes what it finds there, he groans and presses himself into my touch. Then his hands are on my body, sliding up my stockinged calves, past the ribbons at my thighs, right to the source of my desire, which is as slick as anyone studying fluids could hope for. I rub his shaft as he kisses the demi-globes at my bodice. I squirm as he fingers me. Daniel is so skilled that by the time the cab arrives, I have arrived too.

His lab is in the basement of a building at the Academy. It's a large room that smells of dust and chalk, of lamp oil and cold stone. He doesn't bother showing me the equipment. We dropped all pretense of intelligent discourse in the cab. Instead he guides me to an anteroom where there are bookshelves and a writing table. He sits me down on the table. As he fumbles with a lamp on the wall, I rise and creep up behind him so that I can reach around and place a possessive hand on his chest. The other hand I slide under his waistcoat. He jumps at the contact and drops his bundle of matches. We laugh. He chides me for my impatience.

Back at home, my desk chair is getting uncomfortable. Also, I'm recognizing a need for some extra stimulation, so I stretch up to the top of my bookshelf and pull down my vibrator from its niche behind *Fundamentals of Electromagnetism*. My secret friend is an outrageous violet color, but he's nice and quiet. More importantly, he doesn't reek of latex; the mood isn't spoiled if I slide him into my mouth.

But I don't do that now. Instead I imagine that Daniel has lit the lamp and pressed me up against a shelf of musty old journals. His kisses alternate between gentle probes and searing conquests. He finds and then revisits those little spots that get the best reactions, like my earlobe, or the juncture of my neck and shoulder. Obviously the man is no monk, however devoted to his work he might be.

Meanwhile, I knead his ass—should I say buttocks? No, it's an ass. It's a warm, well-muscled ass—and I stroke it underneath the brocade. He in turn has found a spot on my neck that's making me cry out with need. Now my cranny is more than bedewed. It's so wet that a bead of moisture escapes and slips down to my stocking tops.

I unbutton his waistcoat and seek out his nipples—ah, there, no trouble finding something that hard. I pinch them. He moans into my shoulder, but then gets the same idea and lifts my breasts out of the violet silk of my bodice so they're proudly displayed in the lamplight. Then he says all the things that an eighteenth-century man would say about breasts, which nowadays would sound flowery and insincere. But I don't mind. Especially when he begins making love to them with his tongue. No, I don't mind at all.

My pussy is liquid fire now, and I squirm impatiently under his tongue, at last pushing him back against the desk when it's too much to bear. I unbutton his flies and make my acquaintance with his velvet-headed instrument. It is engorged and fairly pulsing with need. I want to taste it, but I also want to watch what happens as I stroke it. Watch his eyebrows arch and a blissful smile appear. Watch him grimace ecstatically. Watch a look of worry flit across his face as he puts out a hand—but no, he's too late. I've achieved my goal, and now I'm treated to the sight of his open-mouthed bliss and his seed jetting out across the stone floor.

I press him close as his trembling stills. Then, experimentally, I brush his lips with a turgid nipple. He fastens on to it like a hungry babe and presses me to him, murmuring endearments. Again his hand ventures beneath my skirts. It's shockingly cool against my feverish quim, eliciting a gasp that fills the tiny room. At first he merely strokes my closed lips, but soon a pair of fingers have worked their way inside. With his trained hands, he draws the fluid out of me.

In my own room, I've long since stripped and retired to bed. My purple wand is working its usual magic, but I'm so excited that I can't keep still. I groan, sigh, tweak my nipples, and writhe around under the blankets. When that's not lewd enough, I coat my fingers with pussy juices and slide one into a place the vibrator can't go. Suddenly I feel the need to have something in my mouth.

So I sit Daniel down on a wooden chair and gather his softened pego between my full lips. My lover gasps in pleasure, but also in surprise; not only that a lady of quality would know of the French art, but that she would practice it with such abandon. I smile around his tool and slowly work it back to hardness. When his manhood stands stiff and tall, he lifts me up and forward. I guess his intent and gather up my skirts. When we settle, all is discreetly covered, but his naked instrument rests against the very entrance to my womb.

It's time. Both of us knew this was implicit in the equations from the start. Now it's going to become explicit.

With a sigh, I sink down onto him. We remain that way for some time—quiet, embracing, mouths meeting in a deep kiss. Then he thrusts, using the leverage from his hands on my shoulders to bring me back down again. We go on. And on. And on until bells ring and stars explode in the darkness behind my closed eyes.

At home, I turn my face into the pillow to muffle my screams. Don't want my roommate to wake up and come bursting in like last time.

The orgasm itself is wonderful—one of those deep ones, where I can feel each contraction and waves of energy radiate from my belly, breasts, and toes. While basking in the afterglow, I remember to let my fantasy couple have orgasms too. They worked so hard to give me mine. Why not be generous?

After a suitable interim, I roll out of bed, put on a robe, and pad out to the kitchen to make myself some tea. The last four chapters of fluid dynamics look complicated, but once my tea and I are installed at the desk, everything seems to make sense. Plus there's this new enthusiasm. I figure if Bernoulli can give me such a good time, his equation deserves a bit of attention.

Nothing of Him
That Doth Fade

POPPY Z. BRITE

THE TWO AMERICANS SURFACED SLOWLY, DIZZY FROM THE SIGHTS of the Great Barrier Reef: the endless billowing vistas of coral, the lone, shy, deadly blue-ringed octopus, the crown-of-thorns starfish still beautiful even as it gradually nibbled away the reef. The boat was nowhere in sight. They removed their mouthpieces, cleared their face masks of water, and looked again. The boat was still gone.

"I think they've left us," said Theo.

"Don't be stupid," said Jack.

They had arrived in Australia a week and a half ago, starting out in gay-friendly Sydney to acclimatize themselves and avoid hearing, at least for a few days, the age-old but tiresome question: *Are you two . . . together?* Neither of them wanted to answer that, not about each other, not any more.

Both were in their late thirties. Theo, a pastry chef, was broad across the shoulders, handsome in the manner of an aging schoolboy, conciliatory unless his patience was stretched too far. Jack, a freelance magazine writer, was long and lean, hatchet-faced and redheaded, always ready with a side-of-the-mouth barb to stretch Theo's patience. They had spent twelve years in each other's company. The first eight or so had been good. The trip was an attempt to recapture that goodness. In his heart, neither believed it would work, but the idea of having again what they'd once taken for granted was worth the time, money, and chance.

It was impossible to put one's finger on the moment when things had begun to go sour between them. They'd never been one of those couples who got along perfectly, or seemed to: even during the first couple of years their fights were frequent, loud, and passionate. Sometimes they reconciled with furious lovemaking. More often they would wake up the next morning and find that the whole thing just seemed silly. They were friends as well as lovers then. Friends could fight, air it out, then put it behind them. Friends could laugh at such things; they had spent much time laughing together.

It was when they stopped fighting that things had begun to atrophy. Now, instead of fighting, they sniped constantly. A shortcoming pointed out here, an old grievance dredged up there. It was a habit that clung as closely to them as they had once clung to each other. Friends did not snipe. But Jack and Theo were no longer friends.

The Sydney harbor threw off azure sparkles. The silhouette of the famous opera house rose above the water like the tail flukes of a white whale diving deep. Jack and Theo chose an outdoor table at a café that promised harbor-caught seafood.

"It's too windy out here," Jack said after a few minutes, weighing down his flapping paper napkin with his knife.

"It feels good. Smells like the ocean."

"Fine." Jack pulled his windbreaker tightly around his lanky frame and huddled into himself.

"Let's go inside," Theo said after a few minutes.

"No, it's fine, you wanted to stay out here."

"You're cold. You're making that quite obvious. We won't be able to enjoy our lunch. Come on, let's go in."

"Don't worry about it."

Theo rose from the table, grabbing his napkin and silverware. "I said let's go in the fucking restaurant!" He turned and stalked through the double doors of the café, not turning to see if Jack followed. After a minute, Jack did.

The combination platter of prawns, oysters, and Balmain bugs was fresh and delicious. Ten minutes after it was served, Theo started checking his watch. "What's wrong?" Jack asked.

"The food took so long to come—if we don't get going soon, we'll miss the one-fifteen ferry over to the zoo."

"So we'll catch the next one."

"I wanted to get there by two o'clock."

"What difference does it make?"

"It's a big zoo. We won't have time to see it all if we don't get there early enough."

"So we'll see whatever we have time for."

"What's the point of that? If we're not going to see it all, we may as well not go. In fact, let's just not go."

"Oh, come on. Where else are we going to see a live platypus?" This was Jack's feeble attempt at a joke. His once-irrepressible wit still occasionally tossed one out, but Theo never laughed anymore.

"We can see one on the Nature Channel back home."

"That's good enough for you, is it? To see something on TV? Figures."

And so it went, over the cracked and sliced bodies of the small sea creatures. As it turned out, they did take the ferry to the Taronga Park Zoo that day, and even saw a live platypus. But neither of them enjoyed it very much.

Two years ago, Jack had discovered that Theo was sleeping with a line cook at the restaurant where he worked. Theo had always maintained that he was bisexual, at least in theory, but the fact that the line cook was a woman made Jack feel doubly betrayed. It was as if Theo had rejected not just him, but his very maleness.

The affair was not serious, and Theo had already broken it off by the time Jack found out. The line cook no longer worked at Theo's restaurant, and Theo swore he didn't know or care where she had gone. Theo and Jack decided to stay together, not so much because they really believed they had anything worth saving as because the idea of being alone after so many years frightened them both too much.

It is said that such betrayals may be forgiven, but can never be forgotten. Jack could do neither. Despite how the memory tore at him—or perhaps because of it—he was never able to let the incident go. For longer than he cared to remember, he pictured Theo with the woman and felt disgusted with his own body, could not bear to look at himself in the mirror or let Theo see him unclothed, let alone touch him. Even now, twenty-four months later, he would hurl it at Theo when Theo was least expecting it, in the most irrelevant situations possible, in the ugliest terms possible. "Oh, I'm not good enough for you because I don't have a pussy. Or tits maybe? Is that it?"

Surrender no weapon, even if it is as likely to blow up in your face as it is to hurt your enemy, even if you realize it is impossible for the battle ever to be won.

The afternoon light on the ocean's surface was a punishing thing, glittering coldly like diamonds, reflecting back up into their eyes. Within a couple of hours their faces were painfully sunburned. Small waves lapped against them, momentarily soothing but eventually turning their skin chapped and salty.

"The boat'll come for us," said Theo. "They'll get back to Cairns and see they forgot us. They'll shit themselves. They'll be back."

"But will we still be here?" said Jack. Theo realized it was a good question; they had no way of knowing how far they'd drifted from the site of the dive.

They had inflated their BCDs and lashed together their empty air tanks, creating an unwieldy flotation device to which they could cling. They linked hands across this device, helping to hold each other up.

"They'll come for us," Theo said again, with less conviction.

More time passed; they could not tell how much. They were very thirsty. They had stopped talking at all. The sun sank lower in the sky, and the water took on a bloody tinge.

Suddenly Jack lifted his head. "Listen," he said, and then they both heard it: the sound of rotors chopping air. A helicopter! They could see it in the distance, a chitinous speck in the gloaming. They both began to shout. Jack let go of the air tanks and struggled in the water, trying to remove his swim trunks. When he had them off, he waved them above his head, a red flag that seemed hopelessly small in the vastness.

The helicopter passed far to their right, circled a time or two more, then headed away. They screamed at it until their throats were raw, even though they knew the people inside could not possibly hear them over the rotors and the wind. Theo laid his head against the air tanks and began to cry. Jack looked at him, then looked away toward where the helicopter had disappeared.

"We could try to swim back," he said.

Theo choked on a sob, tried to catch his breath. His nose was running, and he ducked his face into the water to clear it. "The hell we could. Weren't you listening to the captain? He said the reef was fifty kilometers from Cairns."

"We may have drifted closer."

"Not that much closer. Not possible. And we wouldn't even know which direction to swim."

"We'd go the way the chopper went."

"Which way was that?"

Jack looked around and started to speak, shook his head. He raised his arm out of the water to point, hesitated, then put it down.

"I don't know either," said Theo, gripping Jack's hands more tightly. They managed to heave themselves high enough on the air tanks to lay their heads together, and each felt a tiny bit of comfort, a spark in the cold salt void.

They'd taken a rental car in Sydney and begun the long drive north along the coastal highway, heading for Cairns, the jumping-off point for dive tours of the Great Barrier Reef. Their love of scuba diving was one of the first things they'd discovered they had in common, a thing they had traveled all over the world to enjoy together. They shared a sense of awe for the depths, an appreciation of the sea's majesty that neither of them had ever encountered in anyone else.

It seemed an eternity since their last diving trip off the western coast of Jamaica, but they knew the Reef was supposed to be one of the most spectacular dives on earth: it was a big part of what had brought them to Australia. Driving all the way to Cairns had been Theo's idea. He'd wanted to detour into the outback along the way, but Jack had vetoed the idea on the grounds that it would be full of choking dust, blackflies, and poofter-hating rednecks.

They made good time the first day, driving almost ten hours, then found a room in a small hotel in Brisbane. They had thought to push on the following day, but in morning's light Brisbane proved to be a lovely city, dotted with fountains and sculptures and even a windmill, frosted here and there with lacy ironwork balconies that reminded them of New Orleans's French Quarter. They had last been in New Orleans nine years ago, so the memories were good. They booked their hotel room for another two nights.

The next day they climbed Mount Coot-tha, an easy two-hour hike through slender trees with sunlight slanting through their branches. At the summit, Brisbane spread before them like an exquisite miniature painting, and they could see the rocky humps of islands in the bay. They lingered on the summit and found themselves alone. Jack came up behind Theo, embraced him and whispered in his ear.

"I *do* love you. You know that, you must know that. I'm sorry I've been so awful the past few days. I could never have come here with anyone else."

"Me either," said Theo, and squeezed Jack's long fingers tightly in his own. "Let's just forget the past few days and enjoy the rest of the trip."

They were too tired from the hike to have sex that night, or perhaps they were just afraid of risking the fragile peace they'd forged. But they talked for hours over dinner and wine, the kind of amiable, inconsequential talk they hadn't had in recent memory, and they slept curled tightly in each other's arms.

The car wouldn't start the next morning, though, and they had to wait four hours for a man from the rental agency to show up with a replacement, and they began to snarl at each other again. By the time they had transferred their luggage to the new car and were heading back up the coastal highway, a heavy silence hung between them. The greatest pain was this: each remembered the magic of the previous day on the mountain and the words they had spoken, but none of it mattered.

The owner of Sea Pearl Diving Tours had been dressing down his instructor for nearly an hour, but this did not change the fact that the instructor had somehow failed to do a head count after the last dive. Only when the boat got back to Cairns did anyone realize that two of the passengers were missing.

"Do you realize the odds of finding those people at this point?"

"Yes," the instructor said miserably.

"Do you realize that you will be directly responsible for their deaths if they aren't found?"

"Yes."

"Do you have any idea how much their families will be able to sue us for? You know how fuckin' litigious Americans are!"

The instructor did not answer this last question, as he had no idea how such things worked. He was just a diver who was barely good enough to teach other people the rudiments of scuba diving, but he tried to take care of his groups. The worst thing that had ever happened on one of his dives prior to this was a German woman who had been badly stung by a box jellyfish. She'd been in a lot of pain and mad as hell, but ultimately she had been fine. He doubted the two Americans were going to be fine.

"They're being searched for?"

"Yes, you fuckin' wanker, they're *being searched for*. We've got a helicopter and three boats combing a hundred-kilometer area of sea. A bit like finding the proverbial needle in the haystack, wouldn't you say?"

The instructor wouldn't say anything at all. He only just managed to stand up and get himself out of the owner's office before the hot tears of his shame began to flow.

North of Brisbane, Theo and Jack crossed into the Tropic of Capricorn. The land became brown and scorched-looking, and they had to turn on the rental car's air conditioner, which first worked abominably, then not at all. The tightening fist of the heat did nothing to improve their tempers. The scenery grew monotonous: jagged volcanic outcroppings stabbing into a dull reddish sky. Closer to Cairns there would be dripping, steaming rain forest, but here there was nothing for the eye to rest upon.

They made their next overnight stop in Mackay, the heart of the sugarcane belt that began north of Brisbane and ran all the way up the coast past Cairns. Something about the cane intrigued Jack, and he wanted to explore the town. Theo, who had driven all day, had a pounding headache. In the hotel, he pulled the curtains and went to bed while it was still light. Jack ventured out alone.

He walked through the straight streets, along the windy riverfront, past an incongruously large shopping mall and a sign notifying him that he was leaving the Mackay town limits. Then he was in the sugarcane fields. Cane towered over his head, dark purple, thick-jointed, leafy. The sky was beginning to darken. In the distance he saw a column of smoke rising over the fields, then orange flames flickering through the cane. Somebody was burning off a field before the harvest! Jack had read of this practice, which removed the leaves and was said to sweeten the cane, but he had not hoped for the extraordinary good luck of actually witnessing it, had not even known it was the right time of year.

He stood at the edge of the road watching the fire for a long time. Its fierce color and wild motion drained the sluggishness of the long car ride from him. He did not wish Theo was with him. He felt unusually free, unusually *himself*. Out here, away from his lover of a dozen years, he was only Jack. He was no longer the bickering, blaming Jack of Jack-and-Theo, though he knew he would be that Jack again tomorrow. He realized he hardly knew this Jack anymore, this man standing alone on a country road on the other side of the world from his home, watching sugarcane burn.

For the thousandth or the millionth time, he thought of leaving, of walking on through the cane fields to the next town, of catching a train or a bus back to Sydney. His wallet and his passport were in his pocket. He could go.

He thought about this for a while. Then he remembered Theo's headache; the pain in Theo's eyes had been genuine and slightly desperate. He could not bear the idea of leaving Theo to fall asleep in pain and wake up alone. Perhaps that was only his latest excuse, but it was true.

Jack turned away from the bright flames and retraced his steps back through the cane fields, back into the town, back to the hotel where Theo slept.

*   *   *

Somehow, clinging to each other across the lashed-together air tanks, Jack and Theo dozed fitfully through the night. They were cold when they woke at dawn, but the terrible thirst had eased a little. They both knew it would return in the full light of day.

As the sun rose in the wrong direction across the sky, they saw a plane circling low above the ocean's surface, far away. A little later they saw a boat on the horizon. They shouted and waved just as they had done the day before, but none of it made any difference.

"I'm tired," said Theo. There was a crack in his voice, and at another time Jack might have latched on to that and shaken it like a pit bull. Instead he only said, "I know."

"Do you think we have any chance at all?"

Jack began to answer, but then his head jerked up and his eyes widened. He stared at Theo, mute, obviously terrified.

"What?"

"I felt something brush my leg," said Jack.

They looked down through the clear water and saw huge dark torpedo-shapes circling lazily below.

"Sharks."

"The dive instructor said they wouldn't bother people."

"Yeah, I'd put a lot of stock in what the dive instructor said."

They were quiet for a while, staring down at the dark circling shapes. The sharks made no attempt to approach them, not yet. But the psychological effect was that of a man lost in the desert who sees the first vultures overhead.

"We're going to die," said Theo. It was not a question, not even a half-veiled plea for denial or comfort; it was nothing but a statement of fact.

"Come here," said Jack, and let go of the air tanks.

Jack was already naked. Theo shucked his BCD, kicked off his fins and his swim trunks, and they pressed their bodies together, making a line of warmth in the slight chill of the ocean. The water was a great buoyant hand cradling them as they held each other. They sometimes still had sex, but it had been years since they'd really kissed. They kissed now, softly, remembering the feel and taste of each other's mouths; then harder, with teeth and tongues, with fingers tangling in each other's wet hair.

"You've got a one-track mind," said Theo, and they both laughed. It was something he had said to Jack in the early, sex-drenched days of their relationship, when they could not get enough of each other.

Their hands crept lower, beneath the water line. Their cocks were two rigid columns of flesh. They no longer felt the cold water, had no awareness of the depths yawning beneath them; it was like being in bed together years ago, knowing and feeling nothing outside their world of two-made-one.

They did not trust death to give them that fabled final orgasm. They gave it to each other with their hands and the friction of their bodies, and their seed mingled with the ocean, the salty essence of their lives returning to its primordial home, a triumph over the void as well as an acceptance of it.

Then they held each other very tightly and let the tanks float away. They did not want to be taken, to wonder who would go first, to see each other ripped apart, the pool of blood spreading like an oil slick on the water's surface. Instead, they took one last breath in unison, savoring the seldom-noticed sweetness of air, and dived together forever.

Author's note: This story owes a debt of inspiration to Ray Bradbury's "Interval in Sunlight" and to several works by Harlan Ellison. Thank you to two of the greatest writers America has ever produced.

Watercolor

THOMAS S. ROCHE

VANESSA STRETCHES SLIGHTLY ON THE DIVAN, EARNING A STERN look from Tess.

"Hold still," growls the artist, and Vanessa pouts noticeably. "And don't pout," Tess adds.

"I'm new to this," says Vanessa. Then, with a smirk, "I'm not used to being naked in front of somebody unless I'm *doing* something." The second she says it, she wonders if that was saying too much. *I'm too much of a flirt*, she thinks, and she can feel the heat in her face that tells her she's blushing again.

Tess presses her lips together and looks like she's about to say something nasty. Vanessa feels a wave of sudden fear that Tess is going to comment on the change in her skin tone—surely blushing is the most annoying thing a live model can do. But Tess apparently thinks better of it, and Vanessa struggles to keep still as Tess returns her attention to the easel.

Vanessa's statement is not entirely true; she *has* been getting pretty used to being naked in front of people without doing anything. She's relatively new to the artist's model gig, but she's been doing a hell of a lot of it recently—as much work as she can find. The $10 an hour she gets for sitting naked or partially naked in front of art students sure beats the hell out of the $12 she got for temping in anonymous corporate offices whose inhabitants subsisted by doing obscure late-twentieth-century tasks Vanessa will never begin to understand, not that she'd want to. She's racked up fifteen or more hours of posing every week for the last two months—no easy task, even in a town as artistically inclined as San Francisco. But even for $600 a month—half again her monthly rent, and barely subsistence level—she finds this artistic poverty preferable to kissing corporate ass in the financial district. She's been doing classes at the Art College and community centers, with the occasional drawing club thrown in. And now and then—well, rarely, in fact, actually just this once—the private artist in need of a model.

But all those obsessive students of Vanessa's nakedness are sketch artists, never needing her to remain in a single pose for more than thirty minutes. Tess, on the other hand, is a watercolor artist, and a meticulous one. She insists on working directly from a live model. Vanessa's been in this pose for just over two hours, enough to send into spasms muscles that, until ten minutes ago, the poor girl didn't know she had.

But that's not the real reason the pose is so hard to hold. The fact is, Vanessa felt like squirming the second she took off her clothes in front of Tess, and was tempted to writhe on that red velvet divan. Feeling the heat of Tess's gaze on her naked flesh, lingering on her breasts and belly, caressing her face, it was all Vanessa could do to keep from moaning. It's more than exhibitionism, maybe it's not exhibitionism at all. It's not just sexual attraction—Vanessa gets that directed at her on the street all the time; she learned long ago to completely ignore it. There is something in the intensity of Tess's gaze, the demanding, insistent grasp of it all, that is making Vanessa get wetter the more she lies exposed in the light of the artist's eyes. It has to do with *possession*, about a kind of look that's forbidden in normal parlance.

Working on her painting, Tess can look at Vanessa in a way that just wouldn't be permitted in any other context. She can mold Vanessa in her own image, can recreate the girl on the page. The representation of Vanessa's naked body, a sort of reflection of her interior, can be utterly manipulated and owned by a skillful artist as completely as if she were bound and gagged, stripped naked and lashed to St. Andrew's cross. *Damn, there's a thought,* thinks Vanessa, feeling the heat that tells her she ought to stop thinking like that. But she can't—any more than she can change the form of her representation on Tess's easel in water and color and artist's dreams.

Vanessa never feels this in front of a class full of people—at first she was vaguely gratified that they were looking at her, but there had never been a real sexual content to the gaze. Why is it that she feels this way about posing in front of Tess? Is it just because they're alone in her studio, providing a sort of intimacy? Or is it just that Tess is so mind-bendingly *hot?*

Vanessa tells herself for the twelfth time that that can't be it. Sure, Tess is attractive . . . very attractive. Tess looks like she's in her early thirties, maybe ten years older than Vanessa. She's beautiful, and there's a creamy texture to her skin that Vanessa finds maddening. And she's got that sexy accent—what is it, British? Australian? Vanessa can never tell the difference.

But it's also the sensuality with which Tess works, and the confidence in her movements, that makes her so sexy Vanessa almost can't stand it.

As embarrassed as she would be if Tess knew how turned on she was, Vanessa doesn't want the arousal to end. In fact, she nurses it, imagining what Tess is doing with the reflection of her naked body as the artist's brush dips into the water pot, swirls around the thick paste in the little cups, perhaps grazing the half-formed shape of Vanessa's naked breast, the glistening cleft between her legs.

I wonder what part of me she's painting, thinks Vanessa. Shoulders? Breasts? Belly? Thighs? Calves, feet? Face? Lips?

Throat? Hair? Tess insisted that Vanessa let her long hair down, so it could scatter across the pillow and subsequently across the page. Vanessa imagines the tip of Tess's brush teasing it, stroking it into existence. The way Tess might stroke Vanessa's hair in real life, running her fingers through it as she drew her face closer for a hard, hungry kiss, teasing her lips open the way her paintbrush would open them on the page.

Or maybe, Vanessa thought, *Tess is painting my cunt.* She feels it, all right, feels the touch of the brush on her clit and her lips, not with real sensation but with a body-flushing heat, her cunt reacting halfway between a tingle and a throb. Tess can hardly be painting Vanessa's cunt, since Vanessa's legs are demurely closed. But the thought that rages through Vanessa's head is of lying there on the divan, legs spread as wide as they can go so that Tess can see her pussy, inspect her, *explore* her, and recreate it on the page, taking particular note of the way it glistens in the light, the way it drips on the velvet. Not painting it exactly, not like a photograph, but in Tess's own image. Reflecting her desires, her needs—her lusts.

Vanessa can feel it. She can feel the pressure of the brush teasing her clit, feel what the sensation would be if she were to spread her legs and open wide for Tess's brush, for the fluid touch of the watercolor. For the wet, cold tingle of the brush tip as the brush slips into the shadow there, moistening and changing the heat of that hallowed cleft. Sculpting, caressing, teasing it. Vanessa can almost feel the brush tickling her clit, which she's just sure is throbbing and erect. When she's turned on like this— *really* turned on—Vanessa's clit gets full and rock-hard, harder than that of any other woman she's ever been with. Vanessa feels a certain twisted pride in knowing that she has one of the biggest clits around, especially given her pride that the rest of her is so dainty. More than one lover has commented on the fact that everything about Vanessa is femme except her clit. And remembering the first lover who said that—Alison, another artist, years ago—her attention is drawn right back to her clit, and the wetness Tess seems to be dabbing between her legs. Vanessa knows that brush is going to touch her clit any second now. She knows it's going to tickle her to orgasm as Tess admires and recreates that aching flesh. Vanessa can feel the familiar tingle telling her that her clit's engorged with blood, but she manages— just barely—to fight off the urge to reach down and feel it for sure, to see just *how* erect it's gotten. If for no other reason than because if Vanessa puts her hand between her legs she would feel duty-bound to see just how wet she is, and then things would *really* get out of control.

But she's wet. She knows that much. She's very, very wet— wetter than the glistening sheen on her naked, paper-bound reflection, the one Tess is coaxing and stroking and teasing into life on the page, bringing it to life like Pygmalion his Galatea, bringing it to life all glistening and dripping vibrant, rosy flesh tones. Wetter than Tess could possibly be, unless this is turning her on as much as it is turning on Vanessa.

Is it? wonders Vanessa. *Is this a turn-on for her, too?* She imagines Tess's pussy under that long, flowing, filmy, almost see-through Indian-cotton skirt, imagines it wet and hot, throbbing and glistening like her own. Tess isn't wearing a slip under that skirt, that much was obvious when she walked in front of the window—and Vanessa has to wonder if she's maybe not wearing anything else under there either. Why should she, when she's just sitting around the studio painting? After all, with her models nude, Tess kindly has the heat turned up; it's a foggy day outside. That's why Vanessa is reclining and fantasizing instead of shivering and gritting her teeth, the way she usually does at the cheaper-than-cheap Art College. *She can't be wearing anything underneath,* thinks Vanessa. *Maybe that luscious pussy is just bare under that skirt . . . her legs are crossed, her thighs are spread wide . . . wide . . . spread wide, and her pussy's naked, as wet as mine, just waiting to be kissed . . .*

For the thousandth time, Vanessa's eyes flicker over Tess's pretty face and upper body—and she sees them, sees the firm peaks of her nipples under the skin-tight white T-shirt. *It's not cold in here,* Vanessa thinks wickedly, though of course she knows her own nipples are quite hard and it's certainly not because she's cold—but rather because she's *hot.* Vanessa toys in her mind with those firm, inviting buds. They're just begging for her to put her wet mouth on them and suckle watercolor sustenance from Tess's pretty tits. *Her nipples are hard, hard as a rock. She's probably turned on. She's probably hard and wet, just like me. She's probably not wearing anything under that skirt.* The thought of Tess's body so close and available makes her shiver.

"Too cold?" asks Tess. "Should I turn up the heat?"

"No." Vanessa laughs. "I'm fine."

"You're sure?"

"Absolutely."

I'm being silly, Vanessa tells herself, trying to shake off the fantasy as the artist's gaze continues to move slowly, torturously, over her nude body. *I don't even know that she's a dyke. I don't even know if she's bi.* This must be nothing new to Tess—the walls of her studio are covered in watercolors of naked women, of every possible body shape, color, and size. Vanessa stretched naked in front of her is nothing surprising, nothing new. Vanessa is just flattering herself to think that her naked body was somehow different, somehow more exciting or arousing than all those others Tess has painted. Hardly.

But wouldn't it be nice . . . if she were wet under there? If it were turning her on, stroking her brush all over my body? Teasing my clit with it . . . teasing my nipples . . . slipping it into my pussy . . . ? Wouldn't it be nice if she were thinking about touching me with her hands . . . her mouth . . .

Suddenly Tess cocks her head, as if she's heard something from the other room in the main part of the house. Tess turns back to Vanessa, smiles fetchingly, almost seductively. "Just a minute! Don't move—I'm almost done. I'll be right back!" Tess bounces up from her chair, turns and runs through the door to the house, closing it behind her—but not before Vanessa has seen, with the twirling motion of Tess's body, that it's true, she's really *not* wearing anything under that skirt, and it's just a small leap from there to the idea that Tess's pussy isn't just naked, but *wet,* and with that Vanessa feels a shudder go through her whole naked body.

Alone in the studio, she can't stop herself. Almost before she knows what she's doing, she's parted her thighs slightly, then with a rush of surrender spread them wide on the divan. Her hand has slipped between her legs, her middle finger feeling the firm, erect nub of her clit—even harder than she'd expected. And God, touching it feels so good—a quiver goes through Vanessa's body, and she strokes her clit up and down several times before letting her hand slip down to her pussy—testing to see just how wet she's become.

She's wet, all right. She's incredibly wet. Dripping. Two fingers slide inside her easily . . . then three, with only the slightest effort, something she almost never does when she's alone. She can feel her pussy tight and hot around her three fingers as she pumps them in, juice dribbling out over her palm and onto her wrist. God, it feels so good. She knows she could come in half a minute, maybe less, if she'd just rub her clit and let her fingers do their business. Should she? Vanessa can't decide, and she finds herself just lying there spread on the divan, fucking herself with one hand and rubbing her clit with the other, getting closer . . . closer . . .

Then she hears the chiming of Tess's anklet, and about ninety percent of her wants to just lie there spread for Tess to see as she enters the room—but the other ten percent prevails, and Vanessa quickly slips her fingers out, twisting her body quickly back into the best approximation she can manage of the pose she held before.

Tess closes the door behind her, sits back down in front of the easel. She frowns and shakes a finger at Vanessa. "You moved, didn't you?"

Vanessa feels a flood of heat go through her body, and she swears to God she could come right now if Tess just looked at her some more. But she doesn't, and instead Vanessa laughs nervously and drops her eyes to the ground. "Sorry," she says. "I had an itch."

Tess shakes her head sadly. "What are we going to do with you?" Vanessa has a few ideas. "Well, that's all right. I'm almost finished. And a good thing, too—my husband just came home. We have theater tickets."

The single word sends a shaft of ice up Vanessa's spine. *Husband.* God fucking damn it. Husband. Everybody has to have a husband. Vanessa tries to keep herself from bursting into tears, tries to tell herself that Tess still might be bisexual, still could be just as turned on as Vanessa was. It's possible, isn't it?

But that word, *husband,* has taken the heat out of Vanessa's body, the smolder out of Tess's gaze, the slick, luscious wetness out of Tess's pussy. Vanessa can almost taste the artist's salty tang, a tang she now knows she'll never get to taste in real life.

"It's a damn shame," mutters Vanessa, only realizing after she's said it that she's spoken aloud.

"Hmmmmm?" asks Tess.

"Oh, I was saying it's a damn shame," Vanessa quickly blurts. "I'm really enjoying posing for you."

Tess's brow furrows. "Really? Aren't you getting tired of sitting there?"

"Not at all," says Vanessa. Her voice has an edge that she wishes it didn't, but there's not a whole lot she can do about it. She's disappointed—crestfallen, really. She knows it's stupid, but that doesn't change it. "I love posing for you," she says quickly. "I can't wait to see what you've painted."

"All right," says Tess, pushing her chair back from the easel. "Come on, then. It's finished."

Vanessa's glad to have a distraction from her disappointment. She excitedly walks over to the easel and stands naked behind Tess, careful to keep her wet and fragrant hands behind her, unable to stop herself from admiring the slope of the artist's slim, muscled shoulders.

The painting is breathtaking.

Vanessa's never been painted before—not nude. She's seen sketches: dozens, hundreds of faceless sketches drawn by the faceless students at the Art College and the Mission Drawing Club, hundreds of naked Vanessas sprawled or standing on the page. But she's never seen herself in paint, and certainly not in watercolor—so different, so muted, so strangely evocative. The shape of Vanessa's body is shocking to her, and she suddenly feels that she can't be that naked, she can't be that lovely. And she's not, she suddenly realizes—but Tess has painted the naked Vanessa in her own image, and it's the fluid, watery melding of the two women that spreads across the page, vibrantly lovely in a way Vanessa could never hope to be.

"What do you think?" Tess is smiling faintly.

Vanessa is speechless for a long time as she stares and stares at her idealized reflection. "It's lovely," she finally says, dumbly, wishing she had something better to say. "It's really lovely," she adds, and realizes that the water filling her eyes is ready to dribble down her cheeks. She quickly touches her forehead, as if running her fingers through her hair, but not before a single tear has traced its path down her cheek and onto her breast. Tess's eyes have followed it, Vanessa sees, but neither woman acknowledges the tear.

"I'd like you to have it," says Tess, softly, tenderly, almost the way you'd talk to a lover after sex. "I always give the first painting to the model."

"No," says Vanessa, too quickly, betraying the urgency she feels, the desperate need to own the painting, such a fragile and dangerous representation of her own soul. "I couldn't." But Tess sees it, sees the desire in her model's teary eyes, and she laughs.

"Nope! You have to take it. Take it or I'll be horribly insulted and never let you pose for me again. Understood?"

Vanessa has nothing more to say; she just nods sadly.

"Great. Well, it'll take a bit to dry, so why don't you get some clothes on and I'll make some coffee?"

Once Vanessa is alone again, she wonders at the lack of desire she feels to finish fucking herself. Her cunt's still wet, even her clit's still pretty hard. But there's something missing from it all, so she goes behind the white shoji screen and slowly, miserably puts on her clothes, the long cotton skirt and the Louise Brooks T-shirt and the black cardigan. She laces up her purple Doc Martens as Tess comes back into the room carrying a bamboo tray with a carafe of French-press coffee and some chocolate-covered biscotti.

Vanessa eats four of the biscotti.

Riding home on the bus, Vanessa finds herself feeling foolish again—not that she ever really thought she and Tess were going to end up in bed together; her weird little fantasy just got out of hand. She didn't expect to be so disappointed. But maybe they *did* sleep together, sort of—and the result was tucked away in Vanessa's black rubber backpack, a moment of desire fixed in watercolor.

Maybe that's why the first thing Vanessa does when she gets home, after muttering the minimum necessary pleasantries to her roommates, is to disappear into her room and prop a chair against the lockless door. She takes the watercolor out of her backpack and sets it on the bed, unable to take her eyes off that surprising rendition of her naked body as she slowly strips off her cardigan and boots, lets her skirt and slip crumple to the floor around her feet, slips off the T-shirt, shrugs off her bra and panties. She leaves her red argyle socks on, because the heater's broken. She's not shivering, though, as she climbs onto the bed, facing the painting, looking at herself there on the page, the image more beautiful than she can ever hope to be. Or *is* it?

Thinking more of the artist than of herself, Vanessa kneels, legs parted wide, her left hand sliding gradually down over her breasts, fingers caressing as her palm teases first one pink nipple, then the other, erect. As her hand slides down her smooth belly past a sparkling silver navel ring and finds its place between her legs, Vanessa gasps slightly, finding her clit too sensitive to the touch, as it sometimes is when she gets really turned on but doesn't come for a long time. With gentle, teasing strokes of her middle finger, she feels the blood rushing in an aching torrent into her clit, making it harder and more sensitive than before. She slips one finger into her cunt, finding it still appreciably moist. Vanessa strokes herself with her left hand as her right snakes out to the cardboard box on the nightstand and flips off the lid. She takes out the curved lavender dildo and sets it beside her on the bed before returning for her vibrator. Vanessa doesn't take her eyes off the painting as she props herself up on three pillows against the wall with her legs spread wide and the watercolor between her feet. The dildo goes in easily, her cunt having lubricated itself even quicker this time, eager to resume what was denied it earlier. Vanessa pushes it in and moans softly, knowing that her roommates will hear her if she makes too much noise, but not really caring. She works the purple dildo in and out of her cunt, eyes wide and fixed on the painting, on her own naked body, as she remembers Tess's paintbrush roving across it, remembers the almost tactile sensation of the brush teasing her clit. She pumps faster as she remembers the caress of the wet brush on her nipples. As she tastes the bitter watercolors on her lips and her tongue, as Tess slips the brush into her mouth. As she lowers the thickest of the brushes between Vanessa's spread legs, easing it into Vanessa's hungry cunt, pushing it home and fucking her with it.

Vanessa's already climaxed once by the time she turns on the vibrator and touches it to her clit. Her second orgasm explodes through her body with all the force of her pent-up desire, and she comes three more times before she finally slumps to the bed, dildo still tucked between her thighs, watercolor cradled in her arms.

She thinks to herself, as she drops off to a contented sleep, how it's not really surprising. It's not surprising that a girl like her, so hungry for change, would want to be recreated like that, at the hands of a lover who knows every curve, every crevasse of her body. She's certainly experienced it before, albeit in different ways. The only problem is that this time, the painter isn't a lover.

Or is she?

Vanessa happily ponders that thought in the fading recesses of her conscious mind, the shape of her naked body sprawled billboard-sized across her quiet dreams.

Three days later, Tess calls Vanessa while she's in the bath. Lounging in the hot water, delicately holding the portable phone and trying not to drop it in the bath, Vanessa listens, amazed, as Tess asks her to pose for another watercolor, the next afternoon if it's convenient. Vanessa laughs uncomfortably, a laugh that ascends rapidly into a giggle, and she feels like a fool. She thinks up a dozen excuses, a dozen things she has to do. Then, nervously, she accepts the invitation for the next afternoon. "You're an idiot," she tells herself as she skids the phone, in disgust, over the bathroom floor. But she has a smile on her face as she says it, and then she playfully plugs her nose and descends cheerfully into the warm envelope of the comforting water.

Movements

MICHAEL HEMMINGSON

I. SUITE FOR AN END TO A MARRIAGE

The first time I saw my wife fucking another man, she was by our Jacuzzi the night of The Party. I was fairly convinced it would be the last party we'd throw as husband and wife.

Actually, she was with two men. One was a fellow I didn't know and he was fucking her from behind—his large, hairy hands tightly grasping her hips in an attempt to control the backward thrust of her pelvis as if she were a wild animal. The other one (my best friend) had his dick in her mouth. She was taking this dick down her throat pretty deep, and he was no bigger than myself. She never did that for me. Maybe she never liked my dick; and this is something I could believe, given the recent sour circumstances of our marriage.

"I don't think I'm in love with you anymore," she told me three months before. I was trying to have sex with her. Her pussy was dry like a dry cunt. Finally she pushed my hand away and said she didn't want to. We hadn't made love in quite a while.

"What do you mean?"

"Is it hard to understand?" she said. "How can I illustrate it any better? *I don't think I'm in love with you anymore.*"

"I see," I said.

"No," she said, "you don't."

We tried the marriage counselor routine, and that only proved to drive us further apart, snickering at all the flowery, New Age suggestions the counselor was trying to sell us.

"What a fucking waste of money," my wife said.

Her name is Beryl, by the way.

I stood there, looking out the kitchen window, and watched Beryl fuck. The one who was my best friend, his name is Art.

I wasn't surprised. The night seemed to be heading for this. Beryl was on the warpath to have sex with someone—other than me.

"I'm feeling frisky tonight," she said when she pulled me aside during The Party.

She was drunk. I told her so.

"So I'm *drunk,*" she said, "and I'm feeling *good.*"

I wasn't feeling good. "Thanks for the information."

"I just want you to know," she said, "that I might do something *wild,* I might do something *sexy,* and I don't want you to get in the *way.*"

"I won't," I said.

"I don't want you to get in the way of my being *happy.*"

"I won't," I said.

It started, I suppose, with her dance—or striptease. She put on some electronic music, the kind that gives me a headache. I don't know where she got this music. She began to dance, and had an audience of men cheering as she lifted her skirt and flashed her panties; when she opened her blouse and exposed her tits. She had small, pointed, brown breasts. She was a tall, slender woman with long legs and tanned skin and straight blond hair, a very appealing woman to many men.

"That's some wife of yours!" someone said to me, slapping me on the back.

"Yeah," I said.

Beryl had stripped down to her thong. Drunken hands groped for her. One pair of hands belonged to Art. Beryl giggled and ran out back and jumped into the Jacuzzi.

Watching her fuck, I knew it was the hottest sight I'd ever viewed. It was better than watching a porno: this was real.

I wasn't the only person watching, either. Several men, some I knew, some I didn't, moved toward the threesome. I moved with them. We were all like mesmerized cattle.

Two months ago I was sitting in a bar with Art. We were on our fourth or fifth drinks.

"I think Beryl and I are getting a divorce," I said.

"You think?" Art said.

"Probably," I said. "She doesn't love me anymore."

"*No.*"

"Yes."

"*No.*"

"She said this."

"Do you still love her?" he asked.

"I'm not sure," I said. "I think I do."

"What went wrong? You two used to be the happy fun couple."

"I'm not sure," I said. "I think she might be having an affair."

"You *think?*"

"I wouldn't put it past her."

When Beryl was done with Art and the man I didn't know, she started having sex with two other men. The Party was becoming something else. Other people departed—old friends giving me strange looks. Someone said, "You didn't say this was going to turn into an *orgy*." It was past one in the morning anyway, the time for most parties to start winding down.

Art, with his clothes back on, passed me.

I grabbed his arm.

"Hey," he said softly.

I just looked at him.

"We should talk," he said.

"Yeah," I said.

The Party was over, people were gone. Four A.M. I lay in bed, listening to my wife taking a bath. The door was unlocked. I went in. She stared at me. She was sitting in the tub, water and soap all around her. She started to say something, I held up a finger to stop her. I unzipped my pants and showed her my hard prick.

"Do you plan to do something with that?" she said.

"I have some ideas," I said.

"You look all worked up."

"I am that," I said.

"I haven't seen your dick that bulging and red since . . . since we first met."

I approached her, my body shaking. "Did you like fucking those men tonight?"

Softly, "You know I did."

"I could tell. I haven't seen you fuck like that since . . . since we first met."

She said, "Did you like me fucking those men?"

I grabbed Beryl's head. I was fast and she was surprised. I pushed her face into my crotch. I bunched up her slick wet hair in my fists, like I was angry. I was more horny than angry, or on a fine line that crosses both conditions. She took my cock in her mouth. I wondered how many loads of come she'd swallowed this evening. Mine would be just another. Beryl pulled my pants down and grabbed at the flesh of my ass, yanking me forward, so that I was partially in the water with her, getting wet . . .

In bed, I asked her how long she'd been fucking Art. I knew that tonight wasn't the first time—the way they were with each other: that familiarity of the body. Beryl said, "For a while now."

II. SONATA FOR A NEW PHASE IN MARRIAGE

The three of us were in the Jacuzzi. This was inevitable, this had to happen; I knew it, Beryl knew it, Art knew it.

We'd had dinner. It was a quiet dinner. I savored every bite of the mushroom sautéed chicken Beryl had prepared, the scalloped potatoes that reminded me of being a child and eating Mother's well-cooked meals. It was a warm night. Beryl suggested we relax in the Jacuzzi, drink wine. Art wanted beer. Beryl drank wine. We got naked, acting like excited, modest teenagers doing something daring and naughty, and went into the water.

It was a clear night out, a lot of stars.

I was also drinking wine.

"That's Mars up there." Beryl pointed at the sky, to a bright star with a red tint.

"Think there's life up there?" Art said.

"Mars? Or elsewhere?"

"Mars."

"Sure," she said.

"What do you think?" Art asked me.

"As long as they don't invade us," I said, "I don't care."

"I'm glad you're not mad," he said.

"I'm not mad," I said. "I keep telling myself I should be. But I'm not."

"It's good that you're not," Beryl said. "It means you're growing. It means you're moving in the direction I am, and that makes me happy."

Art waded through the water in her direction. She giggled. He backed her against the Jacuzzi wall. They kissed. I sipped my glass of wine and watched him kiss her. I watched him lift her body up, sit her on the edge of the Jacuzzi, spread her legs, and go down on her. Beryl liked this. She ran her fingers through his wet hair and made familiar sounds of pleasure. I knew those sounds like a distant cousin one has fond memories of. She leaned back, propping herself on her elbows, and let Art work his tongue between her legs, his hairy hands rubbing her stomach and breasts. She looked at me and said, "Come here and stick that dick in my mouth."

I got out of the water. The hair on my body was matted, I was dripping. I liked walking about like this, my cock pointing the way. I crouched before Beryl so she could take me in her mouth as Art continued to eat her pussy, grunting sounds coming from his throat.

We then moved away from the Jacuzzi to a lounge chair, where she sucked on us both: Art and I standing close, almost touching, Beryl going from one cock to another. I could smell Art's body. I could smell the musk from his crotch, and I wondered if I was emitting any odors he could sense. Needless to say, the smell of sex permeated the immediate air around us.

We took turns fucking my wife. Art went first. I wanted to watch them; watching them made me want her all the more.

"Whore," I whispered in her ear when it was my turn.

"Yeah," she said, "talk dirty to me."

When we went to the bed, Beryl wanted us both inside her at the same time. "One in my kitty," she said with a seductive voice, touching herself, "and one in my booty."

"I have hope for us," she said later.

We were lying in bed alone. The sex had been good. I remembered a night, not a month ago, when we were in bed together and she had said, "We should just have wild sex right now, that'd solve all our problems," but neither of us could do it.

"That's good," I said.

"I really do." She kissed me.

I kissed her back.

"I feel so sexual, so alive again. I want to fuck more men. I want to fuck *a lot* of men. I love you. Will you help me do this?"

She could have done it by herself, or with Art, but she wanted me involved, and I wanted to be involved. And Art, of course, wished to be there too.

It started with the gang bang. Art made the arrangements for this, being the resourceful fellow that he is, getting the guys Beryl had fucked at The Party together for another go at it. There were nine of them in all, more than I had originally imagined. Had my wife really fucked nine men that night? I suppose so. Ten, including Art. Eleven, including me.

If I should ever think that what happened was just a wild fantasy, or a dream, I have the evidence on videotape. It was, yes, Art's idea to capture this night for posterity. When he suggested it to Beryl, she got this wild look in her eyes and said, "Yes." I was beginning to know that look better and better. I wanted her to say no. I wanted her to say no because I liked the idea myself.

(A number of times, alone, feeling lonely, thinking of the life I once had, I will put that tape into the VCR and watch. I will watch my wife fuck all those men in a single session, fucking in every combination possible.

Others have watched her. Hundreds, thousands, all over the world. This is really what this story is about.)

It was Art's idea—again—to create a Web site and place stills from the gang-bang video on it. He created the Web page and allowed people to access it for free. In a matter of days, the site was getting thousands of hits. Art said this was a combination of posting stills to various news groups with sexual themes, and the help of a number of search engines.

After a month, he—or we—announced that the whole video-tape could be purchased for $34.95.

In a matter of weeks, two thousand orders came in.

First we were just some people doing kinky things, and now we were in business.

We were, I guess you can say, pornographers.

III. SOLO IN THE JACUZZI, WITH MEMORY

I was alone in the Jacuzzi. It was another clear night. That red star was indeed Mars. I stared at it. I wanted to go there. I wondered what sex life was like on Mars.

In the bedroom, in the house, Art and Beryl were fucking. He had been fucking her in the ass when I had left, and came out here, turned on the jet streams, and sat in the warm bubbling water. I closed my eyes while looking up.

In the water, I thought about the two of them. I pictured his cock going in and out of her butt, the muscles of her sphincter contracting with each thrust. As I thought of this, I started to become aroused. The image in my head was far more enticing than returning to the bedroom and seeing and smelling it. In my mind, I was the director, I was in control, and I made my own movie of the act.

I also pictured scenes from the night of The Party.

I touched myself. I had my cock in my hand under the water, and I began to jack off.

I watched my semen clump in the water and float to the top, getting caught in a whirlwind of bubbles, spinning around, blending in with water and chlorine.

* * *

INTERMISSION

How We Met

I met Beryl at the recital of an experimental cellist; he was on tour for his new CD. In the first half of his performance, he presented classical pieces by Debussy and Mozart. I had difficulty listening—I kept glancing at the blond woman who was sitting alone, across from me in the small concert hall. She was wearing black slacks and a white cotton blouse. She kept looking at me as well. We talked during the intermission. Small talk: *what do you think of the cellist? Oh, he's good.* We sat together for the second half, and the cellist presented his own iconoclastic work, hooking his instrument to microphones, adding special effects, or playing along with a tape full of strange sounds. Toward the end, he did a manic solo and broke two strings. After, I asked the blond woman—Beryl—if she'd like to go get some coffee. "No," she said, "but how about a beer?" Two months later, we were living together. Six months later, we were married.

IV. QUARTET

"We've been approached with a business deal," Art said on the phone. Beryl and I were on separate phones in different rooms, listening together.

"Go on," she said.

He said, "There's this couple—here in the city—who have a successful on-line business. They do the same as us: sell videos and pix of them fucking, or the wife fucking some guys. Then they started to make and distribute vids of other couples. Acting as distributors, growing their business. You know. They came across our Web site, and they want Beryl. I mean, they can sell five times the amount of videos we do. Or so they say."

"What does this mean?" I said.

"More money," Art said.

"More money," Beryl said, "sounds good to me."

This couple—Fred and Donna—invited the three of us for dinner to talk about the possibility of a business venture. Art drove in his own car and was late. Beryl and I were both nervous and we didn't know why.

They had a nice, modestly furnished suburban house, not the kind of place you'd think a big Internet porn outfit would be located. Fred and Donna were also the kind of couple you might see at a PTA meeting—almost conservatively dressed, quiet, and friendly. They were in their late thirties, attractive and unassuming.

Over dinner, we talked about our lives, not sex.

I wondered why I was here. I was expecting drugs, hard booze, triple-X love acts.

Fred suggested we go to the water.

They also had a Jacuzzi, but this one could fit ten people. It was very nice and spacious. Fred and Donna disrobed before us and got in. Donna was a bit on the chubby side, but had a magnificent tan and silicone-enhanced breasts. Fred, I was quick to notice, didn't have a hair on his well-muscled body, and his dick had to be ten inches long.

Art stripped and jumped in. Beryl and I took our clothes off slowly, still uncertain, and joined the party.

We were all drinking champagne, by the way. It always begins with some kind of party.

"You have a great body," Donna said to Beryl.

"Thank you," Beryl said.

"I'd love to fuck you," Donna said.

"I'm not bi," Beryl said.

"Too bad," Donna said. "But maybe Fred can fuck you. I like to watch him fuck other women."

"Sounds good to me." Beryl laughed.

"You got a look-see at his tool?" Donna said.

"Oh yes," Beryl said. "I wonder if I could take it."

"It takes some getting used to," Donna said. "His cock is very nice."

"Yeah," Beryl said.

Art and I looked at each other.

"Let's talk business," Fred said.

"Let's," Art said.

"This past year," Fred said, "we've cleared three million in sales."

I almost choked on my champagne. Beryl did.

"You're shitting me," Art said.

"No," Fred said.

Donna smiled. "We'll make more each year."

"Porn is the backbone of e-commerce," Fred said, "and the amateur market is in a boom. A huge boom. There are dozens, hundreds of people like us making a living off pleasure. We have something many people out there want."

"Intimacy," Donna said, "and love."

"This business saved our marriage," Fred said. He drew Donna close to him. They held each other. They kissed. "We wouldn't be together now," he went on. "It added . . . excitement. It delivered us from an absolutely dull life, the same thing day after day. You know what I mean."

"I was ready to leave him," Donna said. "I wanted something more."

"We both did," Fred said.

"And we found it," Donna said.

Beryl and I looked at each other. I moved to kiss her. She kissed me. Art looked away.

"We like what you have," Donna said.

"We can get rich together," Fred said.

"I like the sound of that," Beryl said.

"Me too," I said.

Fred said, "So let's fuck and seal the deal."

We all laughed.

"Hey, buddy," Fred said to Art, "there's a camera in the house, and a light. Why don't you get it."

Art nodded and got out of the water. He looked lonely, walking away wet and naked. I can't say that I felt sorry for him.

Donna moved to me, and Beryl moved to Fred. I took Donna's large breasts in my hands and rubbed them. Her pink nipples were pointing at me. Beryl was stroking Fred's big dick and she said something like "Oh my." He sat on the edge of the spa, and Beryl did her best to take him in her mouth.

"You want me to suck your dick too?" Donna whispered. "What do you want me to do? I'll do anything, anything."

Art set up the camera.

Donna and I got out of the water to fuck. I had her on her back, her thick legs on my shoulders. She smelled strongly of perfume. She reached up and bit my nipple as I fucked her. Beryl was still sucking on Fred.

"Hey," Fred said, turning to me with a smile. "I think I'm about to come in your wife's mouth."

Art didn't join us. As he operated the video camera, he jerked off. He was now an observer. I could see it on his face: something was missing. He looked lonely and I didn't care.

V. EPILOGUE

Our hair was still wet when we got in the car. We were electrified. The sex had been good, the idea of success even better.

I touched my wife's face.

"We don't need Art," she said.

"I was thinking the same thing."

"Our marriage will work, won't it?"

"I hope so."

"We can be as happy and wealthy as Donna and Fred."

I wanted to say that we *were* Donna and Fred. We'd just made love to our mirror images, and it was caught on tape.

I started the car.

"Turn on the heater," Beryl said. "I don't want to catch cold."

I did, and as we drove, the warmth started at our feet and moved up our bodies and to our faces. We were holding hands the whole way.

Home, our hair dry, we went into our own Jacuzzi and fucked in the water and under the stars, and there was only us, and it was very nice again, for a while.

The Little Mermaid

CECILIA TAN

WHEN I WAS YOUNG, A WISE OLD SEA COW TOLD ME OF THE four elements: water, earth, fire, and air. At the time I had laughed, for I had never known a world other than the watery kingdom my father ruled, the softness of kelp beds and the caresses of the currents. I could not imagine what she described, her great green eyes focused on a place far away, the hardness of earth, the burning of fire, the lightness of air.

All that changed on the day I came of age. On that day I swam to the surface, as every mermaid must do when she seeks her heart's desire. I thought it a joyous day, and yet I could taste the salt of my father's tears in the water as my tail swept me from him, far and fast.

When I came up on the surface the first time, I saw the spray fly into the moonlight like pearls. The Moon! I called out to her with a sea song, having heard so much about her as a child. She smiled down on me and I swam on my back, feeling the rush of foam over my skin. So this was air! Air tickled and made my nipples pucker where they broke the surface. Air fondled and teased as it blew this way and that.

In the moonlight I saw a great shape across the flat surface of the sea. It groaned and I swam closer to it. From my place in the water I could see its shape, so similar to one my sisters and I had found cracked open at the bottom. A ship. And then I heard another sound, shouts and voices.

Far above me, leaning on a railing, was one of the most beautiful creatures I had ever seen. He had a face like a comely merman's; his hair shimmered gold in the moonlight. He wore a white shirt and a circle of gold across his brow. He stood back from the railing then, tall and upright, and shook his shoulders as if he had leaned there too long. He walked along the edge of the ship on long and stalky back flippers.

I waved, but he did not see me, his eyes fixed in the direction of a far-off shore.

I followed the ship as it continued toward that shore, as the clouds gathered and covered the moon, and as the storm began. As a daughter of the sea I had nothing to fear from the waves, but as the storm built, the ship was tossed. And as sea and sky battled, the ship split apart, and men spilled into the water like sand from an overturned shell. I could save but one, and I found him struggling for the surface. I calmed him with a sea song and buoyed his body with mine until the storm passed and a rosy dawn lit the sky.

When he woke, we floated near his destined shore. I lay on my back in the water with his head cradled between my breasts, humming softly to myself.

"I'm dead and gone to heaven," he said to himself as he opened his eyes. "And you're an angel."

His hands crept along my ribs and caressed my nipples as gently as the breeze. His legs hung down in the water, one on either side of my tail. He blinked as if he expected to wake up at any moment. Then he leaned his head toward mine and kissed me.

If his touch was like air, his kiss must have been fire. It started like a current of warm water, flowing down my body from my mouth to the tip of my tail. But as his lips and mine moved across each other, the warmth became almost unbearable, until I knew what I felt was burning. The sun rose then, a ball of hot fire in the sky, and I cried out with an ecstasy so intense it hurt.

"Is this a dream?" he said then, brushing his fingers along my cheek. His arms circled my shoulders, and I felt his body against mine where my tail met my torso. He pulled his legs together as I turned us in a slow circle, and he pressed firm against me as a part of him became tall and upright and as hard as I imagined the earth to be. I wanted to feel him press harder, but in the water we slid past each other too easily. I locked my arms over his spine and took us in to shore.

The waves obliged and carried us up onto the sand, where I felt the weight of his body settle onto me. We kissed again, and as the sun blazed hot on my skin I held him tight. I had never felt such pleasure or agony as the way I burned for him. His eyes were closed now as his hips rocked like a boat on the waves, groaning like the ship with each sway. But this wasn't right, and I knew it. The burning was deep inside me now, where neither of us could touch. We rolled in the edge of the surf, and I looked at the part of him that stood now like the mast on the ship. The yearning part of me knew I wanted to have him inside me, and I knew of no other way than to open my mouth and drink him in. He gasped as I slid my wet mouth over the hardness that was his essence, and I nursed upon him like a hungry calf at a sea cow's teat. Then came a wave of saltiness that was the taste of home.

He gasped and blinked then, and looked up into my face, then hastily down at the rest of me. He stifled a cry and then rolled to one side, hands clutching at the wet sand. "You, you're a . . ."

He said no more as a voice from up the beach came to us then. "What ho! Who's there?"

More people on stalky legs were up on the dunes, and they began shouting as he stood. I dove into the water, knowing somehow that I should not be seen there on the sand. I was still full of the burning, but knew I could not stay. Does not water quench fire? I dove deep, but still I burned.

I came after a time to the cave of a sea witch, an old mermaid who had spent so much of her life at the bottom of the sea that her hair was green like kelp and her skin glowed like a jellyfish. And I asked her if there was anything she could do to ease the pain I was feeling.

"Pain, is it?" gurgled the sea witch. "What sort of pain?"

I described to her as best I could how it felt like hunger, only it wasn't in my stomach, it was lower down; how it felt like fire, only it didn't harm me.

"And does it ever feel better?"

Here I hesitated. For I knew the one time it felt like pleasure was when I was with him. So there was nothing else I could do but to tell her of my golden-haired man from the ship.

"Man from a ship!" She cackled, and schools of small fish darted away from her. "Oh, you poor thing, there be only one thing to ease your pain then." She dove into her cave and came up with a shell. She carefully pried it open to reveal a tiny blue pearl. "Swallow this," she said, rolling it into my hand.

I asked what it was, but all she would say was, "The Pearl of Desire. When you find what you most desire, you will have it. But in trade you will give up the two things that made you one of us, your tail, and your sea song."

But of course I swallowed the Pearl, because I could not know then what a price it was to pay. I swam back to the shore where I had left the man from the ship, but there was no sign of him. I went along the coast until I came to a cliff side. In the moon's light I could see a palace built above the water and the flickering of firelight, dancing bright like my desire. I swam into a calm lagoon toward the sound of voices.

I watched from the water as a man and a woman emerged from the darkness of the trees. It was he, and my heart leaped in my chest to see him. He had a crown of flowers upon his head and his white shirt had been replaced by a patterned cloth around his waist. He pulled the woman down to the sand and pushed the cloth aside, and I could see then what I had wanted so inexplicably before. The hard part of him, rising like a finger of coral. "Come here," he said to the woman.

"My prince, we should not," the woman replied. "If the princess finds out . . ."

"The princess is busy just now," he said, his voice liquid and low. "And I am on fire."

So he too burned. My breath came in quick gasps; the air seemed to fill my head as I watched him turn her body over, as I watched her legs spread.

I pulled myself up out of the water then, and as my body emerged from the lagoon I felt like a sword was cleaving me in two. But I bit back my cry of pain, as I felt the breeze in the space where my tail had been, where now there was a hungry, burning mouth.

Up the beach I heard the sound of shifting sand as someone ran. And then a soft curse.

He was sitting alone, his arms on his knees, his jaw as hard and set as a stone.

I opened my mouth only to find I could not speak. I had no sea song to seduce him with this time. So instead I crawled toward him.

He looked up to see me and his eyebrows knit together as I came near.

I tried to remind him of the sunrise—I touched my nipples as he had, gentle like the breeze. I rolled onto my back and opened my legs to feel the cool air fanning the burning need there.

He did not ask any questions then, did not even pause to kiss me. Instead, he heaved his body over mine and sank that long finger of flesh into me, pinning me to the sand. It felt like a sword cleaving me in two, but then water flowed from somewhere in me, and the fire melted into warm pleasure, and he dove and plunged into me until we were both quenched.

While we lay upon the sand I marveled at the creation of man. Hard like the earth, burning like fire, gasping for air, then leaking the water of the sea through his skin. He looked at me looking at him and laughed. "What is it, my darling? Are you going to scold me too?"

I shook my head.

"No? I finally escape the cold and chill of the mountains, my father's sour temper, and the admonitions of the priests, to be married to an island princess so my father can rule the shipping lanes, and what do I find? Her people may not wear much, but they are just as afraid of lust as mine. Maybe more."

He paused as if waiting for me to say something. When I did not, he went on. "You look familiar. Have we met before?" He squinted at me in the light of the moon, then said to himself, "Must have been a dream."

I touched him on the shoulder to prove to him I was real. He laughed again. "Can you believe I was rescued from a shipwreck? I thought I was dead, but I had this dream . . ." He looked over his shoulder toward the flicker of torches beyond the trees. "A lustful dream . . ."

He pulled me to my feet and it felt as though pins and needles were being driven through my skin. But I smiled and took a step to follow him, to be with him.

"Can you speak?" he asked then. I shook my head. He nodded to me then, smiling, and his smile made me as warm as the sunrise.

I followed him through the trees, up the hill, to a wide terrace of hard stone. "Look, everyone!" he cried. "Look what I've found!"

People came running from inside the palace bearing more torches, all of them dressed as he was, with bright cloth wrapped around their bodies. "My prince!" one of the men said, "where did she come from?"

A woman came out of the crowd and wrapped a cloth around my bare skin. "She must have been in the shipwreck also, the poor thing. What is your name?"

I could not say a thing.

"She's still in shock from being half-drowned," said a man.

"So beautiful!" said another.

Finally the prince quieted them with a gesture of his hands. "Yes, yes, she was on the ship with me. In fact, she was my maidservant, and I'd thought her lost with the rest of the hands. She will be my maidservant again, once she regains her speech. Isn't that right . . . Emerald?"

I nodded, not knowing of what he spoke, only knowing that he seemed to want me near him. And to be near him was all I wanted then.

The prince came to me again in the morning. He had his own quarters, a wing of the palace all his own. I had slept in a bed as soft as any kelp but as light as air, and then had gone to the bathhouse, where hot water sprang up from within the earth. Again I was amazed to find water, earth, fire, and air all in one place. And again my prince came to me, and I tasted his salt with my tongue and took him deep inside me. I could wrap my legs around the trunk of his body, and then even if we slid into the steaming water—which we did—I could still have him inside me. "My salvation," he breathed into my ear, as his flesh spear plunged into me, as I squeezed him hard. "And so you rescue me yet again, from my own burning need."

I wanted to tell him what pleasure he brought me. I wanted to ask him about this land. I wanted to tell him that everything was new to me and to ask him his name. He lifted me out of the bath onto the wet stone and I felt the roughness of his beard like sand between my legs. His tongue wriggled like a fish as it nestled into the soft spaces there and sparked the fire of my desire again and again. With another sudden rush of pleasure like a plunge into deep water, I clamped my knees around his head. But I had no voice to cry out with.

That afternoon I was taken to see the princess. Women came and dressed me and braided my sea-tossed hair. They were very grave as they led me to her chamber, or perhaps they did not wish to speak and remind me I was mute.

The guard there was about to open the door when my prince came running up to us.

"You must not enter, my lord," the guard said, stepping in front of the door, his arms crossed over his chest. "You must not lay eyes on the princess until the day of the wedding."

"Where are you taking Emerald?" he asked.

One of the women who had dressed me looked up with dark eyes. I wondered if this was the woman he had tried to take on the beach last night, for she fixed him with a hard stare. "She will not be harmed," she said. "The princess merely wishes to . . . inspect her."

My prince stepped back, then went back down the hall toward his rooms.

The princess sat upon a throne of fine polished wood worked with gold and silver, and wore elaborate layers of cloth. The throne room was round like a cave, the slatted windows letting a sea breeze blow through. She looked over my white skin, which had seen the sun only once in my life, yesterday, and nodded. She turned to the woman who had spoken to my prince.

"She cannot speak?"

"No, not a word," the woman replied.

"She can tell no secrets then." The princess sat back in her chair, her eyes on the far edge of the room.

"So it would seem, my lady."

The princess waved her hand, still not looking at me. "If the barbarian cannot wait a week, let him plant his seeds here. No one shall speak of it."

I was returned to him.

And so it went for seven days and seven nights, during which I whiled away the hours either in the bathhouse or in the air-light bed, waiting for my prince to quicken, waiting to have my newly empty spaces filled in a manner so intimate I would never have imagined it possible before. The household was busy, preparing for the wedding. The cool white halls were filled with the scent of meats being roasted on the beach, and servants with heaping baskets of fruit went back and forth. From the prince's window I could see men erecting a roof where the wedding would take place. But my prince had no role in these preparations, and we spent long hours lying in the bedclothes. He would slide a finger over my shoulders, down my arm, or use a small palm frond to brush and tickle my newest and most sensitive skin, between my thighs.

On the seventh night he came to the room bearing a basket with food for me as he always did, but he did not feed it to me as he had before. He put the basket down and took me in his arms immediately. The torchlight flickered in his gold-spun hair, and his kiss ranged down from my lips to my neck, then to my breasts as he pulled the cloth away from me, as his lips and tongue moved hungrily over my skin. My hunger for food was forgotten as I drank in his touch instead. He lifted me off my feet and brought me to the bed. I lay there a moment, watching him emerge from his clothing like a crab from its shell. Naked and new again he came to me, his skin on fire and his eagerness for me making his breath shallow. I matched his hunger with mine, gobbling up his maleness as I had that day on the beach, the hard pole of him going deep into my mouth. But soon he pulled me away with a shudder, before the salt spray could come. He hooked one of my legs over each shoulder, folding me up so that the burning slot between my legs was lifted for him.

He plunged a finger into me and I gasped. "You know," he said to me, "I had not known many women before you. I had dreamed of them, desired them, hungered for them, but had tasted so few." Here he bent his head to lick me, and I tensed with pleasure. "And the few who would give in, desperate serving wenches looking for a way to better their position. Dirty sluts. I feared their diseases and their plots for my bastards." His finger returned to the empty place in me and burrowed there. "But then there you were, delivered to me by a magic prayer. A virgin, clean as the sea water running off your skin, and you took me in." Now he heaved himself up to lay his manhood onto my mound. I felt it there, heavy and hot, and it twitched like a fish. He seemed to have no more to say, and into me he dove. How many times had he been inside me since that first night on the beach? More times than I had digits to count. And yet I lived for that moment when we were as close together as two bodies could be. Even as my arms clutched at his back, I held him tight, inside, and he cried out. I felt the salty flow that always reminded me of home.

He slept then, and I would have too, but I heard a song borne on the sea breeze through the window. I heard my sisters singing down in the lagoon, and walking on my pins-and-needles feet, I made my way down to the water. There they bobbed, their heads just far enough above the water that I could hear them.

"Sister, sister, come back to us!" they cried.

I shook my head, unable to say anything else.

"We spoke to the sea witch," Mara, the oldest, told me. "And she told us what she had done."

"But she did not tell you everything," Lara, the youngest, said, salt tears welling in her eyes. "She said you would lose everything if you joined with him."

"Your tail, your voice . . ." said Sara, my closest sister.

"But she did not tell you what would happen if you lost him!" Mara swam closer to the shore. "Only while he is yours will you live. If he gives his heart to another, you will die."

Lara wailed. "We begged her that it not be so. She should have told you."

Sara held something out of the water. "So she told us there is one way you might be saved." She tossed the thing which flew slickly through the night air to land near my aching feet. "Take the knife. If you cut out his heart, you will live. Let his blood drip over your legs and you will grow a tail again. Swallow his blood and you will regain your voice. And then you can come back to us."

"Emerald?" The prince's voice came from above me on the terrace. And my sisters disappeared with a quiet splash.

"Here you are," he said as he approached. The tips of his fingers brushed my cheek, and I leaned my face into the dry smoothness of his hand. I took a deep breath of his salty scent and licked his palm. "Hungry again, are we?" he whispered. My lips found his neck, and the soft place behind his ear, and I felt the fire in him begin to burn again. The breeze itself was a caress on my bare flesh, the rush of the waves a seductive song of its own.

He slid his fingers into my hair and it felt as if I were diving into a clear lagoon, my hair swept back from my face and my body tingling with his touch. Our lips met, and it was like the moment when I broke the surface for the first time, his breath mingling with mine. I could feel his heartbeat everywhere along his skin.

We let gravity take its course, as it so easily did on earth, and soon our legs were entwined on the sand. I could feel the hard barb of him, the stone that I hungered for, sliding back and forth to find its way inside me. And I knew, somehow, that my sisters were wrong. In that first fateful moment when we had kissed, in that first spark of fire inside me, in the first breath of air we shared that fanned the spark to a flame, in that first embrace of the weight of the earth, I had lost the purity of the water. I could not go back. I could no longer live without air and earth and fire.

I cried out as he sank into me, salt tears tracking my face and my feeble feet drumming on his back as I tried to drive him deeper and deeper in. Tomorrow he would marry the princess and I knew, if I did not have his stone to hold me, I would float away into the air. If I did not have the salt of his come, I would burn away to ash. If I did not have his breath to fill my lungs, I would be buried alive. If I did not have his burning desire to draw me up again and again, I would drown. Tomorrow he would marry the princess, but for tonight, I was whole.

In Deep

SIMON SHEPPARD

UTILA'S JUST A FLYSPECK ON THE MAP OF THE WORLD. IT LIES right off the Honduran coast, one of the Bay Islands, a place settled by pirates who braved the seas for gold.

These days, the island's wealth arrives with young divers who come to explore the coral reef. These days, visitors don't arrive by frigate; they fly in from La Ceiba on small planes, planes with warning signs written in Russian, decommissioned junkers from Aeroflot or someplace. Every time the plane dips its wings toward the Caribbean's blue, the passengers hold their breath and pray. I know I did. Except for the praying part.

I'd been to Guatemala already, spent a full-moon night among the pyramids of Tikal, communing with ghosts, getting over a love affair I never should have allowed to drag me down. I'd submerged myself in Kate, her desires and her life and most of all her needs. And after two years of misery, I'd discovered it was a mistake. She was a mistake, my job was a mistake, my life was going nowhere. I decided to skip the worst of a Philadelphia winter and head to Central America to lick my wounds.

The flimsy little plane managed to touch down on Utila's grassy airstrip, just beside a crystal blue harbor. It was only a short walk to the main street. Quaint as hell, wooden buildings, tropical paradise. Dive shops. Restaurants. Lots of small hotels. Hotels without a single room for rent.

Semiexhausted from dragging my backpack up and down the street in a fruitless search for a place to stay, I collapsed into a tattered wicker chair in the lobby of Lucie's Hotel.

"Hey. You look exhausted."

I looked up. He was dark and slightly stocky, Greek background maybe, wearing shorts, flip-flops, and a raggedy T-shirt.

"I am. You know of anyplace to stay? I'll be damned if I can find a vacant room."

"You should have caught the earlier flight over."

"Now you tell me." I grimaced.

"Listen. There's a second bed in my room, if you don't snore. You'd be welcome to spend the night. I'll just have to check it out with the management."

"Lucie?" I asked.

"There is no Lucie. Never has been, I hear." He extended his hand. "My name's Aaron."

"Thom," I said. "Pleased to meet you. How long you been here?"

"A while. Great place to dive."

"So I hear."

"Water's so clear you can always see the bottom. All the way down."

I spent the afternoon settling in, exploring the little town. Half the families in town had the same surname, Harrison. And half the businesses were dive shops.

It was a great place for scuba, all right. Or at least a bargain; prepurchasing ten boat dives brought the price down to a third of what it would have cost stateside. I found a likely-looking dive shop, the Neptune, checked it out, and paid for the ten dives, enough to keep me busy during my planned week on the island.

I was at the far end of the main street when the sky began dumping rain. Everything was getting that wet-tropics smell as I jogged back toward the hotel.

I made it back, soaked to the skin, and went to my new room to change. I was sitting on the porch overlooking the harbor, listening to the rain hammering on the corrugated metal roof, when a blond woman came up the stairs. She wasn't bad-looking—a little plump, maybe, but she had nice breasts, and her nipples showed through her rain-damp T-shirt.

"Hello," she said, her accent Scandinavian. "You just arrived?"

"Yeah, this morning." I was thinking about how one of those nipples would feel in my mouth. I hadn't had a woman since Kate had left me.

"You stay at this hotel?"

"Yes," I said, "I'm doubling up with a man named Aaron."

She made a strange face.

"Anything wrong?"

"No, it's just that I've heard . . ." Another mysterious look. "Never mind."

We chatted for a while about approximately nothing, the way that strangers on the road do. I kept glancing at her tits, I guess.

I finally decided to pop the question. "Are you doing anything tonight? Want to go for a drink?"

"I should tell you," she said, "that I am a lesbian."

And that was that.

That night I went for dinner at a restaurant down the road, the food tasty but served at a snail's pace. It was Saturday, so the town's two discos were cranking up their sound systems, blasting bad music into the balmy tropical night. I popped into one and, by the time I'd finished my first rum and Coke, had decided it wasn't really my scene.

I headed back to the hotel and curled up in bed. I'd had to get up early to make the trip from the mainland of Honduras, so I drifted off quick.

Something woke me up.

I looked around. In the dim blue moonlight, I could see that my roommate, Aaron, had returned. He was sprawled on his back in the other bed, a few feet away in the small room. The sheets were tangled around his feet. His hairy body was naked, and he was jerking off.

I hadn't watched guys jack off since Boy Scouts and I was kind of curious. Careful not to draw his attention, I watched Aaron as he stroked and squeezed his dick. His technique, I noticed, was very different from mine; I tend to really pound away. He was more poetic, slow, like it was happening underwater.

I felt, to my surprise, my own cock getting hard. Not embarrassment, not shame, just surprise. I would have reached down to my crotch, but I was afraid he'd see me. So I lay there scarcely breathing for three, four, five minutes as he played with himself. Every once in a while he'd take his hand away to get more spit, and I could see his cock was very hard, not very big, and gleaming wet.

Eventually he started writhing and arching his back, moaning loudly enough to wake me up if I'd been asleep. With a muffled groan, he oozed a big load of come onto his belly, then wiped it up with his hand and licked it off his palm. He pulled the covers up, rolled over with his back toward me, and seemed to go to sleep.

The next morning I woke up in a sticky little puddle. I never had jacked off the night before, but my come had made an escape anyway.

Aaron was already gone. I was up early enough to go on a morning boat dive. I grabbed a cup of coffee and a slice of coconut bread at a nearby bakery. I thought about the night before, then tried not to. I figured it wouldn't happen again. I slurped down the last of the coffee and headed for the Neptune Diver Shop.

Even without reservations, I had no trouble getting a place on the morning boat. I pulled on the rented dive gear, the wetsuit tightly hugging my body, grabbed my two full tanks, and headed for the dock. There were four other customers on the boat: a married Canadian couple, and a dreadlocked blond surfer from Southern California and his purple-haired girlfriend. The divemaster, Bernd, briefed us as we headed southwest of the island to Stingray Point.

The Canadians had just been PADI certified, so we took it fairly easy on the first dive, only heading down to thirty feet or so. The water was glorious, the coral beautiful, the reef fish streaking colorfully around our group. It had been months since I'd last been diving, and now I remembered why I loved it so: the astonishing peace of the liquid world, the feeling of being where people weren't meant to go, the cold isolation of breathing the air of life through a mouthpiece gripped between my teeth. The beauty of the reef system, which in Honduras is pretty damn overwhelming. Lettuce coral, brain coral, pillar coral, elkhorn, and star. And the schools of angelfish, parrot fish, chromis. The second dive, at Jack Neil Point, was just as nice, even nicer, as big sea turtles swam among our little group. When Bernd led us back to the boat, I was sorry to leave the water. I was sorry to get back to life.

But it was time to head back to shore.

Two dives a day is usually plenty for me. I had a lunch of fried fish at a little place run by two sisters, then went back to sit on the hotel porch and read and catch up on writing postcards. People came and went, sometimes making small talk. I wondered where the Scandinavian lesbian was; I would have liked to ask her more about my roommate, but she never appeared.

It was late afternoon before I saw Aaron. He headed up the stairs and climbed into the hammock suspended from the porch.

"Having fun?" he asked.

"Yeah, went on a couple of dives this morning."

"Explore the island yet? Out by Pumpkin Hill?"

"Nah," I said. "I figure there'll be plenty of time for that. I'm feeling really lazy today."

"We should go out there sometime," Aaron said, "you and I."

"Uh, okay," I agreed.

"Thought about dinner yet?"

"It's early."

"Yeah, but the service is so slow. And sometimes if you don't get to a place early, they run out of whatever you want."

I looked out at the Caribbean, ripples glistening in sunlight. "That's the thing about coming to a place like this. You gotta remain flexible. How long you been here?"

"I'm going to go lie down in the room. Come get me when you're starting to get hungry. After dinner we can go get drunk at the Bucket of Blood."

Dinner was good, the conch soup excellent, though, as Aaron had warned me, the service was glacially slow, even worse than the night before. By the time we'd paid the check, it was well into the night. Over at the Bucket of Blood, we drank rum and Cokes till I had trouble seeing straight. The dreadlocked surfboy was there, looking glum. I wondered where his purple-haired girlfriend had gotten to. For someone who'd been on the island a while, Aaron didn't seem to know anyone there. Which was okay; he was friendly enough, friendlier as the night wore on and we grew drunker. I kind of liked him.

When I'd had enough of cheap rum, strangers, and endless replays of *The Best of Bob Marley and the Wailers*, I suggested we turn in.

We staggered down the street, along with a lot of other soused tourists and a few semisober locals, and stumbled up the stairs to our room. Aaron threw himself onto his bed.

"Oh man," he said. He pulled his T-shirt over his head. "I'm ready to pass out." His torso was fleshy, generously covered with dark hair. He began to unzip his khaki shorts.

"Want me to turn out the light?" I asked. "So you can get some sleep?"

"No, leave it on." He was down to his briefs now. He began rubbing his crotch through the white cotton. I just lay there watching him as he peeled off his underwear and started stroking his cock. He'd thrown his near leg over the edge of the bed, so I had a view of his balls and the hair between his legs.

"Oh man," he repeated. His dick was hard.

And so was mine.

I looked him in the face. He looked back with deep, dark eyes, and nodded.

I reached down and unzipped my shorts. I wasn't wearing underwear; the flesh of my swelling cock was hot to the touch. I pulled my shorts down and my shirt up, grabbed my dick, and started playing with the foreskin.

We lay there side by side, a couple of feet apart, two almost-strangers, masturbating.

I kept glancing from his eyes to his cock, then back to his face. As interesting as it was to see him jacking his dick, it was more intense to watch his face. I'd seen women get off, of course, but I'd never watched another man having sex. I submerged myself in his eyes as he slowly brought himself close to orgasm.

I wanted to touch him, to feel what another man's cock was like, but I couldn't bring myself to do it. And I was half afraid and half hoping he'd get up, come over to me, touch me. But he didn't. So we just lay there, hands working our own hard-ons, until he nodded and said, "Now?"

"Now," I said.

He looked so beautiful when he came. I wondered if I looked that way too. I glanced down; the hair on his belly was strewn with ropes of come.

"Good night," he said.

"I've . . . I'm . . . gonna go clean up, take a shower."

"Don't move," he said. He swiveled himself out of bed, knelt on the floor beside me. He leaned over my torso and gently lapped up my come, his tongue moving over my belly and chest. I wanted to grab his head, part of me did, and guide him down to my dick. But I didn't.

When he was done, he wordlessly got into bed and curled up under the thin bedcover, his back toward me.

After a while he spoke. "You can turn out the light now," he said.

The first thing Aaron said to me when I woke up was, "Fuck the boat dives. Let's go snorkeling out by the airport."

"Sure," I heard myself saying. We slipped into Speedos and T-shirts and, grabbing our fins and masks, headed out.

It was a shortish way down the street to the landing field. As Aaron and I wordlessly walked side by side in the morning sun, I kept thinking back to the night before, the sight of his cock, the feeling of his mouth on my flesh. I looked over at his face, then down to his hairy legs. Despite myself, I was getting hard. I shifted the fins in front of my crotch, but Aaron caught on and chuckled.

"Don't worry about it," he said. "Happens to the best of us."

Beyond the rocky shoreline, the warm Caribbean stretched forever. Nobody else was around. We adjusted our masks and snorkels, pulled on our fins, and walked backward into the gently lapping waves.

Even in the shallows, the waters were alive with riotously colored fish. Careful not to cut ourselves on coral, we swam a little ways out, breathing through our little plastic tubes. The ocean bottom receded with every stroke. Sea anemones wavered in the currents, feeding on things too tiny to see.

I felt Aaron's hand stroking my side. For a second I wanted to push it away. Instead, I hung there, floating on the surface of another world, while his touch explored my flesh. His fingers moved down to the waistband of my Speedos, then over my ass. Kate had never touched me that way; no woman had. He slipped his fingers beneath the thin fabric, touched the flesh of my butt. His fingertips moved toward my ass crack. With a kick of my fins, I jetted myself away from him.

I wanted not to be feeling those things, I wanted my cock not to be throbbing in my bathing suit. I wanted to look at the pretty coral and the pretty fish and forget that I'd ever known Aaron. Instead, I floated in the crystal-clear embrace of the water until he caught up with me. I let him touch me again, touch my chest, my belly, run his hand across my crotch, my hard cock, peel down the front of my suit, grab me, my flesh, my dick. He tugged my suit down around my thighs and dove beneath me. He pulled at my feet till I was vertical in the water, then surfaced for a breath and dove down again. Looking down, I saw him spit out the mouthpiece of his snorkel. Exhaling a trail of bubbles, he wrapped his mouth around my dick, his tongue even wetter than the water. The vagaries of buoyancy dragged us upward till I was on my back, Aaron floating between my thighs, his face now above waterline, breathing through his nose, his mouth still in possession of my cock.

"Jesus, Aaron, somebody might see us," I said, and as if on cue, the drone of the morning plane came over the horizon.

He took his mouth from my hard-on, which flopped onto my belly, little waves lapping at my dick flesh.

"Let's go back to the hotel room, then. Unless you're afraid."

"Let's just go back. Go back and do nothing," I said. "Give me time. I've gotta think."

The walk back was awkward. When we got to the hotel, Aaron kept on walking down the street. I went up to our room, took a cold shower, then went out to stare at the sea.

As I sat on the porch, the Scandinavian girl came up to me.

"You've been spending time with him?"

"Aaron?" I asked.

"*Ja*," she said.

"Just what do you have against him, anyway?" I was sure she could see into me, my dirty secret. I was sure she knew.

"He's no good. Dangerous."

"How the hell would you know?"

"He used to be my boyfriend." Her voice was tired, resigned.

"But you're a *lesbian*!"

"Yes, mostly, but Aaron and I lived together in Chicago. We came here to Central America together last month. He used to be my boyfriend."

"Until?" I asked.

"You'll see," she said.

I was lying on my bed beneath an open window. There must have been a power failure. The electricity didn't work. The fan didn't move. Even with the window open, it was hot and stifling. I didn't care. I lay there, thinking about the shipwreck of my life.

Aaron still hadn't returned when the wind picked up, blowing dark clouds over the island. And then, with that suddenness of tropical rainstorms, it was pouring, coming down in sheets. I could have reached up and shut the window. I didn't.

The rain blew in, soaking me, my clothes, the bed. I didn't care, I didn't give a fuck about anything. I didn't have Kate, I hated my job, I hated my life. I was forced to admit it: the only thing that had given me real pleasure for a long while—well maybe not pleasure, but some interest at least—was Aaron, being with Aaron.

"Enough time?"

Aaron was standing in the open doorway, sopping wet.

"Huh?" I said.

"You had enough time to think about things, to decide?" There was the slightest trace of a sneer.

I nodded. He walked over to my bed, stood in front of me, and pulled down his wet Speedo. His dick wasn't hard, not yet, and somehow that made it all the nicer. I could understand now how a woman could see a threat in a hard-on. I could understand how nothing mattered, really. I reached for him.

Our wet bodies slid over each other. His dick was hard now, and mine was too, and we kissed, the first time I'd ever kissed a man, our tongues like dolphins, our breaths intertwined. When our faces parted, I asked a question. "Now what?"

Aaron slid down over the rain-soaked sheets as thunder drummed outside. I expected him to suck my cock. But he pushed my legs up and slid his face down to my ass. His tongue dove inside me. I was ashamed. But my penis was stiff.

Am I a faggot now? I wondered, as he licked my ass, kissing, tonguing, like some strange fish swimming where it didn't belong. I heard a moan, my own, above the thunder. And then lightning. And his mouth moved to my balls, licking, sucking, till I began to ache.

"My cock, please. My cock," I begged him.

"Suck me," Aaron said.

"Me suck you?"

"Who else?"

"Yes," I said. "I will," I said, then was sorry I'd spoken. But he was already moving over me, twisting his body so his crotch was against my face. The head of his cock, a deep, angry pink, darker than mine, was inches from my mouth. What the hell. I opened wide.

It wasn't bad, sucking cock. A little strange, maybe, but then it got good. I was hungry for Aaron, for his small, hard cock jutting from a bush of curly black hair. I was hungry for him and I gulped him down, as far down my throat as I could without gagging. He pumped into me, rocking back and forth the smallest bit, never leaving the back of my mouth. Rain was hitting my face. I grabbed his ass, held on tight. Rain was hitting my face.

I couldn't breathe. I tried to, through my nose, but it wasn't enough. I wondered if anybody had ever choked to death sucking cock.

"Let me loose, Thom. Back off, you fuck," Aaron said.

And he pulled his dick out of my mouth and slid down till he was lying on top of me, two men's bodies, wet, face to face, dick to dick. He kissed me. Harder, longer than before. I felt his hands go around my neck. If lightning had flashed just then, it would have been too melodramatic. Lightning flashed.

His lips were still on mine as he squeezed down gently on my windpipe, harder on the arteries on the sides of my neck. I should have been scared. He squeezed harder. I was all of twenty-eight years old, maybe about to die, and I didn't mind. I wanted him to keep squeezing. Harder. Harder. He did.

I was straining to breathe. Trapped blood was throbbing in my brain. I was still aware enough to feel our two hard cocks rubbing together, wet. I wanted him to fuck me. He wasn't going to; he was going to choke me. Things looked darkish red, little spots dancing before my eyes. I was out of air. I reached for his wrists, intending to pull his hands away. I grabbed them, all right, but I drew them inward instead. The thunder was close now, rattling everything. I was making little mewling noises, hoarse, tiny gasps. My mouth opened wide for his tongue. I wanted to unhinge my jaw for him, a boa constrictor swallowing poisoned prey.

Things became even darker, dark as night. It was nice. I could feel my eyes bulging out of my skull. I threw my head back, gave my throat to him.

"Oh, yeah," he said. "Oh *man!*"

I thought of the blond dyke with the big tits. I had been warned. Everything went black.

When I came to, struggling to the surface of consciousness, Aaron was lying beside me on the wet bed. My belly was spattered with ropes of come.

"I been unconscious for long?" I asked.

"No, not long."

"And whose come is this? Yours? Mine?"

"Does it matter?" Aaron asked.

"To me it does, yeah." Though I'm not sure I could have put into words just why.

"Both of ours," said Aaron. "You came while I was strangling you."

"Really?"

"Yeah, and so did I." He didn't quite smile.

I wish he'd have fucked me, I was thinking. *At least then I'd know for sure what it feels like.*

"I guess we should close that window now, let the room dry off," I said.

But my bed was still damp when nighttime came around. When it came time to go to sleep, I crawled into Aaron's bed and lay there shivering beside him. He didn't say a word, just wrapped his arm around my neck and gave it a squeeze. My cock got hard.

It was still hard when I woke up.

The previous winter, Kate and I had gone cross-country skiing out West. I'd gotten hold of some cocaine, and we decided it would be fun to ski while we were buzzed. We skied five or six miles to the rim of a valley; the last few hundred yards to the overlook was an icy mess. On the way back, the coke started wearing off. We were in the middle of nowhere when a snowstorm hit. One of my gloves had started coming apart; the snow made its way through the unraveled fingertip, bringing a cold that led to numbness. The storm rose to near whiteout conditions. I was exhausted and lost, and all I wanted to do was give up. I started to whimper. I told Kate that all I wanted, all I could do, was to sit down in the snowy field and wait to die, to freeze, to melt in the next spring's thaw. But she, unsympathetic, had skied on ahead and I had no choice but to follow. Somehow we made it back to the lodge.

I thought about that ski trip on the boat the next morning. Aaron had decided to come along and dive, and as I looked at him I remembered that snowy, helpless feeling.

The boat was heading to the north side of Utila, to the dive site near Blackish Point. The seas were a little rough, so to take my mind off the sway of the boat, I decided it was time to ask.

"I was talking to this blond girl, says she's your girlfriend. Is she?"

Aaron's handsome face battened down. "She's a bitch. A crazy cunt."

I kept quiet after that.

We reached the Point, and the boat dropped anchor. The other divers on the boat weren't very experienced, so Aaron and I had talked the divemaster into letting us go off on our own. We double-checked each other's equipment, let some air into our BCD vests, held our hands over our masks, and launched ourselves backward over the side of the boat.

There's something about the shock of hitting the water that never becomes routine. It's the feeling that your equipment, so heavy on land, has become effortlessly light. The sudden submersion, the bubbles rising from the regulator, the commitment to entering a whole other world for a while.

We made the "OK" sign to each other and let the air out of our vests, sinking down into blue space. Everything was beautiful down below. The choppiness of the surface subsided into a deep, wet calm. We swam side by side, Aaron and I. Schools of fish swam this way and that, reversing direction en masse. The reef was alive all around us. There was nothing to break the silence but the bubbling sound of my own breath. Everything was beautiful. Everything.

I looked over at Aaron, made the "OK" sign again, and got one in return. He gestured to go deeper down. With every exhalation I sank a little farther, till we hovered over a patch of sandy bottom. The usual feelings of diving—being far beneath normal existence, somehow free of gravity, totally in my body yet really nowhere at all. I looked at my depth gauge: ninety feet.

He gestured at me to sit on the bottom. I couldn't see a reason not to, so I knelt on the sea floor, stirring up a little sandstorm. He came over and knelt in front of me, so close that our knees were touching. He laid a hand on my shoulder and we stared at each other through our masks. I could feel my dick getting hard inside my wetsuit.

Then Aaron grabbed my air hose. I took a big gulp of air. He tugged at the mouthpiece. I let him. I let him pull it out of my mouth. I held my breath.

I could die right now, I thought. *It would take so little. Just allowing my mouth to open, letting the ocean rush in.*

Why was I doing this? Trusting him, letting myself believe he'd give the regulator back to me and let me suck in life again.

Letting go. Right here, right now, my last moment. The end.

My lungs began to ache for air.

Relief. The salty water, salty as my blood, bringing an end, a darkness, maybe peace.

I thought of the moment when he'd put his hands around my neck and squeezed. The girl with the big tits was right. Aaron was bad news.

His face would be the last thing I'd see. He would watch me shoot upward into blue shafts of sunlight, only to thrash, relax, and come to floating rest.

I looked upward. The surface was so far above. It might as well have been as far as the stars.

I should do it, I thought. *It would be so easy.*

My body was rebelling. I needed air. Fuck this shit, fuck Aaron and the places he took me and my hard dick and Kate and my life. Fuck it all. I needed air.

I could die right now.

I grabbed for his hand. He let go of the regulator, which floated upward out of reach. Through the glass of our faceplates, our eyes conveyed some primal, elemental message. Older than civilization: animal trust and betrayal. I made the "out of air" sign, fingers slashing across my windpipe. I was going to die. He would never let me breathe.

It would be so easy.

He blinked once, and reached down for his spare mouthpiece, the "octopus." Gently, he held the back of my head with one hand and guided the octopus toward my mouth with the other. I opened my lips, he placed it between my teeth and I clamped down, greedy, breathing again.

He gestured to rise. I could have grabbed at my regulator hose, replaced my own mouthpiece. Instead, I remained breathing through his spare, the two of us sharing the same air as he put his arm around me and, locked in a wet embrace, we rose slowly toward the surface. When it came time for our decompression stop, he put both arms around me and hugged. Then he reached for his mouthpiece and his octopus, gently pulled the regulators from both our mouths, and kissed me, parting my lips with his tongue just enough for a trickle of salt water to rush in.

Then he replaced his mouthpiece, I got my own regulator into my mouth, and we rose toward the surface, toward life.

I needed to go for a walk. I'd come to Utila to escape. To escape my life, but my life had followed me, hitched a ride with me on that Russian plane. If I'd come to Utila to simplify my existence, I'd come to the wrong place. Somewhere out in the middle of the sea, I was walking down the same small street again and again, wanting there to be somewhere to get lost.

I figured I'd finally hike out to Pumpkin Hill. I never got there. The Scandinavian girl was coming up the street, a bag of groceries in one hand. She placed herself in my path.

"The supply boat has come in, and the grocery store has now more food again. Look." She held the grocery bag toward me.

Jesus, I thought, *is this woman everywhere?* And then I realized it wasn't just her; since I had gotten to Utila, I'd been seeing the same faces again and again. Only Aaron was hard to find, always disappearing.

"So what," the girl asked, "have you learned?"

What a fucking weird question. Or maybe she'd been reading my mind.

"Huh?" I asked.

"About Aaron. Have you found out?"

"Found out what?" I didn't want to talk about it. I didn't want to think about it, about Aaron, about me. I wanted to relax, let the currents carry me, watch my thoughts swim off like a school of bright, mindless fish.

"How do you think someone gets that way?" she asked, an odd look in her very blue eyes.

Fuck you, I wanted to say.

Instead I said, "Excuse me. I've got to go." And I turned around and headed back to the hotel before she could catch up. Maybe Aaron would be there.

When he fucked me that afternoon, he didn't use a condom.

"I'm okay," he said.

"Trust me," he said.

I did.

It didn't feel quite like I'd anticipated. A little pain at first, which was to be expected, and then just a funny, full feeling. Once he got going, though, once I relaxed, once he was all the way in, it all changed to pleasure. Sweat was glistening on his chest, dripping off the hairs of his belly.

I wanted him to choke me again, but I didn't dare ask him. I lost my hard-on, from all the new sensations, but that didn't matter much. His pleasure was all that counted. I wanted to be nothing. When he shot off inside me, I hoped I could have been anyone. Even the girl from Scandinavia.

"Stay inside me," I gasped. "Please stay inside me." And I jacked off, getting hard fast, feeling an intense longing, a need to spew salty come everywhere. It didn't take long for me to shoot. Jism arced all the way up to my face.

We showered. There wasn't much to say. I went off to find us a snack. In the heat of the late afternoon, Utila's main street was nearly empty. Walking felt strange; I could still feel him in my ass. It was if my body were carrying some barely concealed secret, something about being looser, more open. I was glad there were so few people out; discovery would be less likely.

When I returned to the room, every trace of Aaron was gone. No note, nothing. I felt resigned, then curious. I ran from the hotel, heading for the airstrip. As I got there, the last plane of the day was warming up on the runway, pointed toward the mainland. As it taxied down the field, I thought I saw Aaron's face at a window, looking toward me, but I couldn't be sure. I stood there, stupidly, until the sputtering roar of the plane faded away over the deep blue sea.

When I got back to the hotel, there was a boy with a backpack at the front desk, kind of scrawny, but cute. His neck was thin.

"You look exhausted," I said to him.

"Know of anyplace to stay?" he asked. "Every hotel seems to be full up."

"There's a second bed in my room," I told him. "You'd be welcome to spend the night."

I looked down at his legs, fuzzy with brown hair, then back up at his face. It would be so easy. "You'd be welcome to spend the night," I repeated.

I caught a trace of motion from the corner of my eye; the Scandinavian girl with big tits was standing there, staring straight at me.

"Hey," the boy said, "that'd be great." So easy.

"This way," I said, and we headed up the stairs.

Minarets

BARRY YOURGRAU

I'M IN A PORT CITY, AMONG DOMES AND MINARETS AND DUSTY balconied hotels. By a shore beloved of conquerors and poets, where water ferries ride glimmering in the murky, lurid dusk.

I'm not alone.

The woman in my life is with me.

My love is very fond of me (and I of her); also, she speaks up about my faults. Such as: my mix-up about which train would get us here.

Or: our hotel room.

"But at least the guidebook was right; it *is* an old, picturesque part of town," I protest sheepishly, after dinner even as before, in the clatter of the fan. "And these carpets and whatnot show fine workmanship."

"What do you know about carpets?" my companion snorts, grimacing. She groans and rolls away on the bedclothes, holding her head. "I feel sick," she complains. "Oh, I shouldn't have had all those figs and syrup! Oh, it's so hot!"

I can't help chuckling tenderly. I hang woozily over her, amused and solicitous. "What're you laughing at?" she demands. I suppress a belch. "You stink of alcohol!" she protests, shoving me and huddling away deeper into the dark pillows. "Thank you, my sweet," I murmur. "Look who's talking," I add, under my breath.

I get to my feet and sway toward the paltry French windows, rubbing my neck. I trip over a bag of her purchases from the bazaar and stagger, cursing, into the wall. She curses from the bed. I reach the windows and belch into my fist, and stare gloomily out at the dim blank alley. Our holiday hotel view, in a city of panoramas . . . From out of sight beyond, a heated breeze stirs the odors of car fumes and charcoal . . . and an almost lascivious, briny sweetness. A sickly pang of yearning ambushes me from out of nowhere. I swallow. I tremble. "Open the window more, it's stifling in here," a half-asleep voice whimpers behind me. "Oh, the room is spinning!" I do as bidden, breathing heavily. I look over my shoulder.

I slink out into the night.

Perhaps I do so just as a brief refuge from a poky room and a few too many sour words. Perhaps for a little more air after too much drink.

But that's not really why I steal along under the wrought-iron street lamps and the balconies, my heart knocking. Something meaner goads me, a lingering grimy despair from the years of being a man and tourist yoked to holiday hotel domesticities. Down the long hill I sway, toward lights of the shore glimmering down below and the fabled wealth of enticements of this hookah-dream port. I walk and walk and walk, craving just a tiny taste of that lurid salted sweetness in the night air.

I find myself at last where I can smell the water yards away. Dark-cheeked sailor types in pom-pommed caps slink out from a lane that winds off in shadowy cobblestones. I run my sleeve over my mouth and glance back up the hill toward my distant hotel—toward the sleeper I've abandoned.

The sleeper and her sharp tongue.

I start onto the cobblestones. A red window beckons. I stare at it, then move along. I pass another. A woman's voice keens in song from a doorway by a pink-lit window . . . a quavering nasal plaint of wrenching intimacy. I stop across from it and gnaw on a knuckle. The lurid breeze pushes me across.

It's a small lamplit tiled room with a dark old bar counter, empty but for a fat, badly shaved barman in his fez. He pours me a drink that turns cloudy from water. I swallow a gulp of its harsh sweetness to cover the thud of my nerves. "Strong—" I croak quietly, setting the glass down. But my attention is elsewhere.

The barman grins. "You like, you want? Go on, beloved, all for you," he coaxes.

"I don't know—what you mean," I stammer. But of course I do. After another fumy swallow I wobble to my feet from my stool, and turn to sway over to the heavy brocaded curtain in a doorway from which the scratchy singing issues. Heart thundering, I push the drapes aside.

"Welcome, beloved!"

A fat, elderly woman in a florid shawl lifts flabby arms in greeting. She waves at me to enter, flashing cheap jewelry everywhere, and makeup like cake frosting. I edge through, staring about warily. I find myself in a kind of den, with a worn couch and cushions and frayed carpets. An old gramophone blares its siren song. "Will you smoke?" wheezes my hostess. She indicates the smoky bulb of a hookah works in the corner, with its trailing hoses. I decline frantically, suddenly in mind of a tourist's drugged nightmare in a notorious port. I blink from the effects of cloudy drink.

"OK, OK, some tea then," she says, hands up at my fuss, crossing to a little brazier. "Before our beauties appear." The words gust through me, raw. "No thanks—well, OK—I guess," I murmur, accepting a steaming glass in a wire-rim holder on a little saucer. I look behind me and sink feloniously onto the edge of the couch, while the old dame crosses to another doorway and calls up a partly hidden staircase. I blow a trembly breath across the tea. The design of the carpet underfoot brings to mind the carpet back up the hill, and a pang of personalized guilt sears me. I douse it with a gulp of tea, which is strong and oily and jarringly sugared.

"Hey, what's in this?" I mumble, grimacing at my glass.

"Here they are," sings out the hostess.

Ankle bracelets jingle. Female flesh fills my glimmering vision as I raise my head. There are two of them, outfitted like belly dancers—barefoot, veiled, and seminaked, with jewels badly wedged in their belly buttons. I stare as they undulate a foot away from me like a low-rent Judgment of Paris for the nearsighted. Or like a seedy, loony vaudeville act: the one on my left, stubby and squat, wiggles away maniacally to the gramophone's lament; her lanky-limbed beanpole partner just shifts from one bony hip to the other. One of the beanpole's almond eyes is badly crossed above her nose veil. Her low-slung breasts shift about heavily in their big-ringed chain-mail pouches.

A worm of grimy lust wriggles in me.

"No . . . no . . . wait—" I gulp, in slow horror at what transgressive brink yawns before me.

I start to struggle up, but my legs go fuzzy. "The tea—" I blurt, thick-tongued. The old dame's cliché laugh goes up somewhere in the wobbling shimmer of the room. The entertainment closes in: chubby fingers and long long slender ones tickle my squirming thighs, flit up my shirt. Warm dusky rentable flesh presses me, and gauzy veils brush my nose in a haze of sickly sweet scent. "No no—please—no don't—" I bleat, and continue to as the scene shifts, as we stagger and giggle up dark stairs and lurch into a dim stuffy room, down onto a pallet of carpets.

"No, stop stop stop—" I plead away in somber primal despair, as the beanpole squats on her trinketed heels at the barely open window, clutching the sill, with me somehow wedged in behind her on my back, fumbling and thrusting from there. Her veiled cheek rests along a hand as she grunts out a slow, ancient beat. A smell like nougat and sea rot wafts in over us. I hear the galloping clank-clank of chain metal violently starting to hurry, and I lose myself completely with a pitiful, drowning snarl of protest.

Giggles erupt beside me from the dimness. My flapping hand is seized, and a pair of its fingers roughly shoved somewhere, to a torrent of squeals.

After a while, I realize I'm being toweled. Then, blinking and swaying, I'm brought back downstairs to lamplight and laughter and *beloved*s. And the bill, which is highway robbery. I pay it without protest and decline the mint that comes with it. The impact on a holiday budget scorches my ribs through my shirt.

I totter back out to the cobblestones and trudge off, hangdog, toward the long incline of the hill. A lone garish light still blazes in a lurid window. Passing it, I manage to keep at bay what's transpired, like someone mentally holding his breath. But once I turn mush-kneed onto the bigger street, the full shock of what I've done engulfs me.

"Sweetheart—oh god, forgive me!—" I bawl, up the dark, deserted hill, toward a grumbling sleeper in her fourth-choice hotel bed.

I slump in anguish against a bouquet of iron railing around a slim tree, a prowling Aladdin distraught at the gargoyle (himself?) he's unpopped. Behind me, the watery lights glimmer in the fairy-tale night, pierced by the lances of the minarets. I whimper, a tea-addled transgressor, overcome by remorse and degradation. I claw at my mouth in age-old despair over what kind of age-old story I could possibly concoct. The seawater whiff of my fingers makes me squeal. I thrust them frantically in the dirt through the railing. I huff up the incline as fast as I'm able under the faint stars and sickle moon, wiping my hands on my pants and feverishly trying to plot how I can clean my culprit self up and somehow manage to crawl into bed without causing a secondary uproar.

All at once I stop, rigid.

I'm missing something, I sense. Something extremely valuable.

My heart drops into my stomach. I clap wildly behind for my wallet in that timeless tourist gesture. It's there. But not so, I realize, staring down in slow, swaying horror . . . not so what there should be: in front. I lurch a half step, aghast.

"I've been—ROBBED! —" I squawk.

I swirl around and back, openmouthed. I plunge my hand chaotically down my pants again, and still find nothing but nothing. I stare, puffing in shock, down the hill toward the waterside.

"Back so soon, beloved?" exclaims the old painted one, smiling broadly as I come plowing through the curtains into gramophone land. Her smile congeals under the spray of my grievance, the ancient counterplaint of the outraged, shame-faced, straying whoopee-maker. When I throw in "Mickey Finn's" and "Calling the police!" for emphasis, her overpainted lips curl into a sneer.

"Why so police—why so police, fella?" she demands, her crusted eyes flashing.

She heaves away from me and comes waddling back with an ornamental tray. "Stupid tourist sneak-arounds, always run off leaving their things behind," she mutters contemptuously. She dashes the tray down onto the couch. "Take yours and beat it," she tells me.

I gulp in disbelief. Before me lies a jumbled lost-and-found of culprit male private anatomies, like a harvest of wrinkled mollusks: some very pale-haired, some dark-spun and tangled, all of them unmoored from their natural habitats. The old dame watches me, arms folded under her shawl, as I swallow and blink and poke about gingerly to find what's mine. My two erstwhile Mutt and Jeff playmates drift in from the stairs and stand looking on somberly. Above their veils they somehow now sport sailor caps, brightly pom-pommed.

"You sure that's right?" the hostess demands when I've made my choice. "Of course I'm sure!" I sputter, clasping the cause of my woes to my chest protectively with both hands. I turn to go, then stop. I redden. "Listen . . . could I, er—use—the bathroom?" I mumble. The old one regards me scornfully. She jerks with her thumb over her shoulder. All at once she grins.

"Perhaps you'd like one of our beauties to help you?" she suggests.

"No—" I squawk. "No no!"

When I'm done with my private fumbling, there's one last complication about signing a receipt. I refuse.

I hobble once more out into the alley, waddling at a grotesque snail's pace, stooped over and wide-legged lest I jar and dislodge things. I moan in desolation, in travail. Above me the night sky is starting to fade at its edges, the fabled pink dawn swells over the low domes and minarets and the lapping shore. The insidious smell of dates and briny tar rises, disperses like a teasing phantom. Finally I just drift, cringing, to a halt, unable to go on; clutching my miscreant head to shut out the words that keep battering with the nightmare of my misbegotten jaunt:

"What happened—where have you been?" demands someone dear to me, shadow-eyed with worry in a poky holiday hotel bed. Faltering, my panting voice stammers out its attempt at an answer.

Hot Springs

CAROL QUEEN

IT WAS SUNDAY MORNING BEFORE I FINALLY GOT OUT OF THE city, leaving behind the piles of books and notes that were my dissertation and closing the apartment door firmly on them. By the time I'd driven an hour north into the valley, I'd begun to relax. The leaves on the grapevines were beginning to turn, great clusters of soon-to-be-harvested fruit everywhere, but the October day was hot as summer. It was beautiful, and got more so after I'd left the valley towns behind and begun the drive up the old wild mountain, the road narrow, one switchback after another, and a slightly hazy vista of hill and valley and hill at every turn. Little enough traffic up there that I could take the mountain curves fast, two-handed, my car and I like one creature. I love this feeling, that I'm half man, half machine. Soon I reached the hot springs.

I was ready for a two-day soak, ready to sleep under the mountain stars, ready to be away. The springs were old sacred land, one place where the vast geothermal soup bubbling under the mountain broke through to the surface, appropriated lately as a kind of New Age resort. Still a powerful place, though, and its proprietors now tried to reinforce that sense of the sacred by dotting the place with little shrines, a Buddha here, a goddess there. Its specialness was most apparent in the demeanor of its visitors, all of whom seemed to sense and respect that it had been a healing place long before any of us were born. I lost no time in choosing a place to camp, then sliding into the warm pool; my dissertation, already well out of mind, retreated a little further still.

I'd left the water to sun myself on the nearby deck when I saw her, unloading her car with her companion. Probably her lover, by the way she spoke to and touched him—familiarly, almost absently, for she seemed more absorbed in her surroundings. A newcomer here. I caught her eye, and she let a small, wary smile slip; then they climbed the steps to the lodge. Not campers, then. I watched them leave their room to explore, strolling the grounds, locating the pools and the showers, passing me once or twice. Then they went back inside. I imagined them undressing, falling onto the bed, making love.

But he was out before long and in the pool, and it was an hour or more before she emerged, clad in a towel. Their room key hung from one of her hoop earrings, and when she turned or shook her head, it grazed her neck, making a tiny jingle, I imagined, that only she could hear. She stepped down into the water. The pool was so deep that as she glided through, the key's tip touched the water, making a little wake.

She stood alone for a while, eyes closed, feeling the warm silk of the mineral springs on her skin. He saw her and moved to join her. Heads close together, they talked quietly for a moment, then left the pool for the sauna. I watched the door swing closed behind them.

He returned to the pool alone. She was probably still inside, probably lying flat on the smooth, hot wood of the benches, the heat searing into her with every breath, sweat pooling between her pretty little breasts—she had a tattoo on one, but I hadn't been able to make it out from a distance. He came in slowly, pearls of sweat on him, too, surveying everyone—surveying me. He moved toward me through the water. Had he seen me watching them?

He smiled, said hello, began to chat. He was gregarious but somehow sweet, with big blue eyes and the smile of a cherub. He asked my name, told me his, found out within a scant few minutes where I was from, where and what I studied, the topic of my dissertation, how soon I hoped to be finished, and what I wanted to do next. He and the woman were indeed first-time visitors to the springs, and they'd heard all sorts of things about the people who congregated here. He talked about his work a bit—he was a nurse who cared for AIDS patients—but more about hers. She was a sex educator, he said, who also did AIDS-related work, teaching people about safer sex. He'd been talking about her for a full five minutes before she emerged from the sauna, prompting an overly bright "Well! There she is now!" from him.

She moved with the languor of one surrendered to relaxation. I could see the sheen of sweat under her eyes in the deepening twilight, and she carried her towel in her hand, not bothering to cover her nakedness as she approached the pool. The key swayed from her ear as she moved. Others in the pool were watching her too.

Did I imagine the look of pleasure when she saw that he was talking with me? She slid into the water and moved toward us, laughing. "You're such a friendly thing, honey," she said, and he laughed too. Then he introduced us, and her attention turned to me. He told her what he'd learned about me; she asked me to tell her more about my academic work, more keenly interested than he had been.

Serious, intense green eyes. She reached to touch him but kept her eyes fixed on me. Her tattoo shimmered below the water. I thought I could make out the images of a moon and a star. Maybe I'd ask her about it later.

"I understand your area of interest is sexuality," I said, imagining the ridiculous, leering way she must have heard it said before, hoping

I sounded nothing like that.

"He's been talking behind my back again, eh?" she said. She smiled at me, arched her eyebrows at him, and he laughed like a kid caught at a game and said, "Yes, I've been telling him all about you."

"I used to read Kinsey out loud to my friends when I was seventeen," she said. "The study of sex always fascinated me, but it didn't seem a serious enough area to specialize in . . . too lightweight, too dilettantish. Until recently," she added, with a little frown.

"Until AIDS?" I asked.

She nodded. "Now it's too real, it's crucial. People seem to have a lot of trouble adjusting to safe sex, or else they're in such fear that they risk losing touch with their sexuality altogether."

What a funny pair they were. He was listening to our conversation with satisfaction, his blue eyes gleaming, looking first at one of us, then the other, not seeming to respond much to her great seriousness. Some sex educators manage to make the juiciest pleasures sound dry and academic. Not her: she talked about sex like it was the grail, a higher calling—passionate yet earnest, like a Marxist talking about revolution. Tempted to make another wisecrack—"Well, I bet you excelled at your labs"—I decided instead to meet her devotion to her subject with the kind of respect I'd want anyone to show about my own work. She seemed like someone I could be honest with.

"I have to confess I've had some of those problems myself," I said. "It can be so difficult to know when to talk about safe sex—and I can't really say I like to use condoms." It seemed perfectly easy to talk to her about it. But he was quicker to reply than she was: "You're in luck—we give lessons!" he said with a big grin. Her smile flashed back but she pretended to ignore him, saying, "The real key is having a casual experimental attitude, especially at first. Take it too seriously and it'll seem like work, not pleasure."

I also pretended I hadn't heard him. I regarded them. Were they coming on to me? Her earnestness in talking, her lack of flirtatiousness, threw me off, though he was certainly forward enough for the both of them. Was she a participant at all? Surely she was not just acting ingenuous. I determined to wait until she extended me an invitation before I decided whether to take it.

I didn't have to wait long. He moved behind her as she and I continued to talk, and lifted her. He held her up with one hand—easily, she was buoyed by the water—and traced her body with the other. She sighed and settled back against him. More of her was at eye level now, her breasts above water. I could see the tattoo clearly, and even in the dimming light, I could see that her nipples were growing hard from his touch and the cool air. It was not immediately clear whether this was a show for me; I felt a little uneasy, not knowing, nor knowing how to proceed. Was I going to be a part of this scene?

He moved a couple of steps closer to me. She was now so near that if my cock were erect—which it was beginning to be—its tip would touch her. She looked me full in the eyes. All of us were silent for a minute. I wondered what she was thinking.

"What about it?" he said at last. "Do you want a lesson?"

That made her laugh again. "You amaze me, boyfriend," she said to him. "You move so fast. Sometimes I think you move too fast." And to me: "Well? Since he asked—would you like to come with us?" Her eyes said, Come with us.

Decision instantly made. I touched her then, running my fingertips up her belly, across her breasts, over the tattooed crescent. She made a low sound. "I would love to come with you," I replied, and he stepped closer again, so that she was held up by the pressure of our bodies on her. I felt four hands on me, and one of her nipples—hard—rubbed one of mine. She squeezed my cock between her legs for a second, then made way for his hand. She sighed deeply. Her fingertips slipped through the hair on my chest, freeing scores of tiny bubbles trapped there; they effervesced between us. He had my balls, holding with just enough pressure to make me want him to squeeze. I sighed too. I wanted to kiss her.

"Let's go before we get scandalous," she said. We carried her through the water, our submerged hands still caressing. She led us back to the room, detaching the key from her earring as she walked, and showed us inside.

Plain room, bed in the center, their things strewn about. The covers already down—she'd apparently been napping earlier—and while she was pulling them down further, he caught her from behind and tumbled her onto the bed, so I had to wait for my kiss. But from their embrace she reached for me.

I knelt over them, wondering where to start. The muscles of his ass were rhythmically tightening as he began to thrust against her, and she writhed against him in response. As he moved down her body, his mouth now on her breasts, she pulled me down to replace him in the kiss. Such hunger. She held my head, one fist curled in my hair and the other pulling my beard, biting my lips, tongue finding tongue.

I might have lost all awareness of everything but that kiss: teeth and tongue and lips, licking and sucking, tiny bites, feeding the heat and the hunger. But he reached for my cock, and in a couple of strokes, it swelled to fill his hand, splitting my awareness between her and him, kiss and cock. As she sucked my tongue harder, he began rubbing my cock head with its foreskin. Wet with pre-come, it almost felt enveloped by another mouth; involuntarily, ecstatically, I thrust harder into his hand, moaned into her.

Feeling me respond to him made her hotter. She answered my moan, though I felt it vibrate in my lips and tongue more than I heard it, for my mouth was still on hers, my fingers teasing her nipples. Her hands did not stay in one place for more than a few seconds at a time; she scratched softly at my chest, tugged my hair, clutched my arms as her arousal heightened.

I broke the kiss when I felt his absence, looking over my shoulder to find him rooting around in one of their bags. "Accoutrements," she said, and in a minute he was back, smiling hugely, to roll one condom onto me and one onto himself—his erection, by now, making him look more like Priapus than a cherub. He took my cock into his mouth.

And sucked, near-perfectly. Like an angel. It was just right, and I moaned again, couldn't help it. He was jacking himself off as he sucked. I could tell he was keeping us both at the same rhythm—too slow to come—our hearts probably beating in tandem. His eyes were closed in concentration and bliss.

Hers were open wide, watching like a cat as the shaft vanished into, then slid out of, the tight circle of his lips. Each time the glans hit the back of his throat, I shuddered with pleasure, and she saw that. My fingers had moved to part her labia and slip inside her sweetly slick cunt, and she sighed and spread her legs to me but didn't take her eyes off her lover, lost to his cocksucking.

"Do you like this? Do you like watching him suck me?" I whispered. I began a slow exploration of her cunt, pushing into her at the same pace he was devouring me, all hearts beating together now. She loved watching, she said.

He heard us, came back to earth a little. Still squeezing my cock, he motioned me to my knees and moved up to her; she saw what he was doing, was already spreading her legs to him and reaching for the lube, and I watched as his rubber-covered dick disappeared into her. Once in, he turned back to me, mouth ready for my cock again. His sucking wasn't quite so perfect now—he had more than one task to concentrate on—but that was more than made up for by the pleasure of watching him fuck her. She was meeting his strokes, thrusting up, still raptly watching the cock-and-mouth dance, sighing and murmuring and moaning softly, and I watched the pink mist of her sex flush spread across her breasts and up her throat, watched her eyes widen and flutter closed as he stopped sucking me and began to fuck her seriously, harder and faster as her orgasm neared. I moved back so I could thrust against his flank and followed his rhythm, imagining we were both inside her, our cocks rubbing together, held so tightly by the silky, wet muscles of her cunt. Maybe she was imagining the same thing; she'd licked her fingers to moisten them and was making fast, purposeful circles on her clit; she was climbing, obviously climbing. I stopped my pretend fuck and reached between their spread legs, my fingers forming a V at the entry to her cunt, adding to the pressure on her labia, and giving him more tightness to push through. Her eyes opened wide for a second, acknowledging the extra sensation, and then she reached her peak and was rocking and releasing into orgasm, crying pretty cries. When she was done, I was there to kiss her into another, heightened hunger.

He began his own climb after rolling her on her side, one leg drawn up to her chest, fucking her even faster, and she knew the signal, for she began a whispered litany as he tensed and bucked: "Yes, honey, oh yeah, come on, come on, baby . . ." And in a soundless orgasm he collapsed onto us, grabbing for my cock again as soon as he could move, kissing both of us at once, which made her laugh.

He rolled off us, and she squirmed more firmly underneath me. At a glance from her, he pulled off the rubber he'd dressed me in before and slid on a fresh one. Then he took my cock and began to slide it up and down her cunt lips, across her clit (I could feel it hard against my sensitive glans), teasing us both by putting it in just a little way and then, just as we began to thrust, pulling out. But he could feel how badly we wanted the fuck; he didn't toy with us for long.

She moaned when I entered her, slowly, thrusting deeply in, maintaining the low song until I began to withdraw, resuming it when I pushed in again. She wrapped her legs around my waist, arching up to meet me, wanting to be filled. She reached behind her head to grasp my wrists, leaned up to kiss me, and the look she gave me was articulate as any words: Fuck me.

Slowly, to tease us both, but I wanted her hard. I could feel her nails imprinting the skin on my wrists; I shifted so that I was holding her wrists, and she caught her breath, moaning, "Ohhh, man . . ."

If she had anything more to say, I didn't hear it; my mouth was on hers again, and she sucked my tongue like he had sucked my cock, and her eyes didn't leave mine. I read her arousal in them like a meter as I took her the way I wanted her: as hard, as fast as I could without shooting too soon. We were electric, thrusting into each other wildly and eyes not parting, and I wanted it to last, freezing time with our heat.

I slowed down long enough to release her wrists and raise her legs to rest on my shoulders. She took my whole weight—and the length of my cock—as deep into her as I could plunge, and she was not silent for an instant now, crying out at a particularly strong thrust, moaning and sighing, saying, "Yes, oh, oh, yes, oh man, fuck me, fuck me . . ."

She slid her right leg off my shoulder so she could reach her clit; she climbed fast. I slowed my stroke a little to make it last. "Ohhh! Oh baby, don't stop, don't don't . . ." I didn't, and I was deep inside her when her cunt began its fast, hard squeeze. She was whimpering, clawing my shoulder, and I didn't slow, thrusting through the hard contractions, seeing her eyes register the pleasure of the first stroke after orgasm as she began to climax again immediately, gasping and then crying out. I rode her through three orgasms before I lost control and shot, holding her tightly and feeling her cunt throb around me like a tight, wet fist.

He lounged next to us on the bed, jacking off. The spectacle had gotten him hard again.

Acting on a decision I didn't know I'd made, I reached for a condom. I hadn't had a cock in my mouth since middle school; I suppose I hadn't given much thought to whether I ever would again. But I was clearly embarked on the sort of erotic adventure with these two that I could never have foreseen, and what's more, I trusted them. What had she said? A casual, experimental attitude? "Use an unlubed one," she said when she saw what I was up to, and I managed to get the rubber on him while she watched, that cat-on-the-hunt look coming into her eyes again; I heard her sharp intake of breath when my lips touched his cock head. I didn't much like the taste of the latex—had a moment of regret for the loss of naked cock skin, even as long as it had been since I'd tasted it—but my mouth slid down the length of it, and I concentrated on the sensations, his cock so hard and hot against my lips. I glanced up: his head was thrown back and he was breathing deeply; she was absorbed in the vision, her fingers almost absently slipping up and down the length of her cunt lips. My cock was starting to stiffen again already; it responded to the look in her eyes as she watched me. I felt the heat of her arousal under my own skin. Energy built between us even as I felt his fast pulse beat on my lips.

He reached for my cock. I reached for her, pulled her down to join me. Together we ran our tongues up and down his shaft, kissing around him, trading our attentions from cock to balls. I played with her breasts, tugging on the nipples, feeling her response. He jacked me off with long, slow strokes.

He wanted to fuck her again. So did I, but I could wait. This time I watched for a while, hand on my dick to keep it as hard as he had left it (I wanted to be in the minute he was out). I took advantage of the lull to change condoms. When I saw her hand move toward her clit, I slipped a finger into her cunt, still thinking of both of us in her at once. So hot and tight, wet with sweet, salty cream. She got tighter when I put a second finger in her, then a third. When I began to move them in and out, her cunt stretched with his cock and my fingers. She began her whispered orgasm-song again, arched up in a perfect Reichian curve, climbing, climbing. I wanted her full, fucked like she'd never been, this tattooed little sex priestess. She held her breath, mouth open in an inaudible cry, until she came, but nodded, eyes wide and on me, "Yes, yes . . ."

And came hugely, once, twice—not enough, and then he stiffened with pre-orgasmic tension; I felt him slow his thrusting the instant before he came.

The minute he pulled out, I was on her, enfolded. And we fucked slowly, tight in each other's arms, soul-kissing, soul-fucking, a long time, a long time.

I rolled her over so she was astride me, and I could watch as my cock slid out of her pussy, and she thrust down on it again. She braced her hands on my chest and rode me, my hands cupping her ass. Then I had her on her back again, closer, faster, to finish.

"Have I only just met her?" I thought. She, silent and intense, gazed at me, engaged in her own wonderings.

They did this all the time, he told me as we all lay in one another's arms, talking, letting the intensity ebb in preparation for my getting up, going out of the room, leaving them.

She had me understand it had been another caliber of experience this time, that it did not always feel like this. Her fingers stayed tangled in the fur on my chest, just over my heart.

Would I leave my number with them? he asked. Could we all meet again?

Of course.

Anyway, it was only Sunday night. We were all staying until Tuesday. Time to play like slick fish in the effervescent water of the warm pool, to meet under the shine of the stars, to talk, catch up in words to this deep knowing. In one another's arms, in the arms of the holy mountain.

Velvet Glove

KRISTINE HAWES

THE BASKETBALL GAME DRONED ON IN JOEL'S EARS. HE DIDN'T really care about the commentary, he just liked to watch the game. With a distant, primal part of his brain, he heard Jessica in the kitchen puttering around. He idly wondered if she would watch the game with him. She hated basketball. She would get distracted, though, and end up with her head in his lap, sucking him off. Her favorite pastime. Joel's cock stirred at the thought of her wet lips, her breasts pressing against his thigh. He shivered. He adjusted his still-growing cock and tried to settle in and watch the rest of the game.

Jessica walked out of the kitchen and down the hall toward the bathroom, trailing her bathrobe tie behind her. Pause for commercial. Joel jumped up from the couch and followed her.

"Here, you're dropping your tie," he said as he picked up the satin cloth and threw it over her outstretched arm. He noticed the towel in her other hand. "You don't usually take a shower at night, do you? How come now?" His thick fingertips lingered on her waist.

"Just feel like it." Jessica smiled. "Care to join me?" Her dusky green eyes caught a glint. She turned her head so her eyes could be seen only through her blond bangs. Her fingers moved up his wrist, his arm, resting finally on his collarbone. A smile danced on her lips. Joel shivered again.

"The b-ball game is almost over. I'd like to finish it. Care to join *me?*" Joel leaned down, kissed her lightly. His hand moved from her waist, up the side of her body, to rest on her breast. He tweaked her nipple quickly.

Jessica laughed, pushed his hand away. "I guess I'll have to take care of it myself then, huh?" She pushed his body back playfully. "Just the shower massage and me." She laughed as she turned.

"Maybe after it's over." He let the phrase hang between them. "Oh, Jess, come on. Please?"

"Suit yourself." Jessica turned and moved off up the hallway. Joel watched her swing her hips just a little more than necessary, her firm thighs and soft ass inviting. She turned in at the bathroom doorway. She smiled, blew him a kiss, and closed the door. *Damn*, he thought. He wanted to see the game—no, he wanted Jess. He could always have Jess . . . The game. His cock pushed against the starchy cotton of his briefs. *Damn.*

Joel, still standing in the doorway to the living room, un-muted the TV. The game was near the end. His mind wandered into the bathroom, thinking about Jessica's brown, smooth legs, the tan lines arcing in a V down her round ass, another V diving into the soft flesh of her pussy. Joel shifted to give his cock room to breathe. He turned the sound on the TV up as the shower splashed on. Jessica's large breasts covered with warm water, pink nipples hardening under the cool spray—he could barely focus. His jeans soon became too tight; he popped the top three buttons. The purple head of his cock peeked out through the top of his briefs. Jessica would be turning now, letting the warm water flow through her hair. She'd be lifting her hands, sluicing the water back from her cheeks, her forehead, pulling her hands back through her hair. Eyes closed, she'd be moaning as the water ran down her spine, into the crack of her ass. His fingers clasped his cock through the thin white cotton, a clear tear of pre-come oozing from the slit. He slid his index finger over the tip and pulled the droplet away, a thin strand of come linking his finger and his cock. He rubbed the head with the slick juice. His cock jumped. *That's it*, he thought. *Screw the game.* What was he thinking?

Joel held up his unbuttoned jeans as he walked to the bathroom door. He heard the faint sounds of water splashing, Jessica's voice quietly moaning. He slowly opened the door and slipped inside. He closed the door again, softly. His cock quivered. He slipped out of his jeans and underwear as fast as he could. He pulled his T-shirt over his head and shoved the clothes to the corner of the dressing area. He moved to the tub, hovering just outside the shower curtain.

Jessica's moans were soft, as if she were trying to hide them. She shifted. He steadied himself as quietly as he could. His hand moved to his thickening cock. The whole shaft was purple now. He let his fingers press down on the underside, the intense sensation sending shivers through his stomach and thighs. His hand slid down, cupped his balls, and pulled them gently. Jessica was panting now. Joel closed his eyes and imagined her finger rubbing wildly over her clit, her other hand pinching her tender, hard nipples. He imagined the water coursing over her skin, making the hot hotter.

Joel's hand moved steadily up and down his shaft, tugging at the silky skin. He pinched his nipples as Jessica's breathing quickened. She moaned louder, breathing heavily. He wanted to wait until she was coming before he got in. His hand worked slowly, stretching out his own pleasure. Jessica gasped, her voice rising above the rush of water. Her cries muffled quickly, as if she had put her hand in her mouth to stop from being heard. Joel's cock pulsed a constant stream of clear pre-come, the head now slippery and wet. *Now*, he thought. *I've got to be in there—now!*

He slid the curtain back slowly and moved into the shower. Jessica's head was pressed against her arm as she leaned against the far wall. Her other hand was pressed between her legs. When the water stopped, she turned. Her eyes opened wide even as her face broke into an embarrassed smile.

"Couldn't wait for me, baby?" Joel smiled. He loved catching her this way. Her hair was slicked back, her cheeks bright red. She was still panting, one leg propped up on the tub ledge, and her fingers still moving slightly.

"Mmmmm. You wanted to watch men play with their balls," she gasped. Half-laughing, she pulled her hand from between her legs, turned, and held it up to his face. "All the time you could have been playing with this."

Joel grasped her hand and held it under his nose. "I love the smell of your pussy," he said. He looked her in the eyes as he licked each of her fingers. Jessica always smelled like cinnamon and pepper and copper. "I love the taste even more," he said between licks. His cock bobbed of its own accord.

Jessica stayed with her back to him as she spoke, her head turned to look at him as she leaned against the tiled wall. She wiggled her ass, pushing her wet skin against his firm shaft. "How about putting that thing inside of me?"

"I'd love to." Joel licked his lips and grasped his shaft, resting one hand on her hips. Jessica leaned forward, her ass sticking out. Joel's cock was so hard that it curved toward him, forcing him to push it down toward her. He moved the head to her lips, yet as he let go, his cock slid up to her ass. Jessica moaned.

"Mmmmm, yes. Would you please?" She moved her ass in a circle, pressing against the head of his cock.

"You sure? We've never . . ."

"Yes, please . . . Fuck me in the ass, please, Joel? I like it that way. A lot." Jessica's voice teased him. His mouth watered and his nipples were tight. Jessica leaned down and grabbed some of the liquid soap. She quickly coated his shaft and stroked him a few times. Again he aimed the head of his cock toward her lips and it slid up to her asshole. "You have to help me," he whispered.

"Mmmm," Jessica moaned. "That's it. Right there. Now push just a little. That's it." The head of his cock felt like it was pressing against a stone. Suddenly her body seemed to give way, opening. The tip of his cock pushed into her tender hole. It was all he could do not to bury himself deep inside. Jessica moved her hips slightly, guiding him.

"That's it. Yes, just a little more," she coaxed. He watched the head pop inside her, ridge nudging past the tight muscle. It encircled him like nothing had before—not hand, lips, cunt, teeth, or condom. Nothing. Joel pushed harder, pressing into her deeper. She took a heavy breath, relaxing. "Keep going, that's it, baby. Just keep pushing inside. Slowly, slowly. Yeah, that's it. Mmmmm." Her voice trailed off into a long, rich moan.

Joel took a deep breath himself. He would come quickly from this if he wasn't careful. His cock was surrounded by smooth, hot skin. He pushed as far as he could, his balls swinging against her wet and swollen lips. Swallowing, he began to pull back, slow and controlled. The shower water was warm on his back, almost too warm. He let his hands rest on her hips as he watched his cock emerge.

"There, stop there. Yeah, that's it." Jessica was almost cooing. "Now, again. Push inside me again. Please, oh, god." Joel began a slow rhythm as he watched his cock open her ass to accept him. The tight rings of muscle soon loosened, yet constantly held him as he moved past them. He focused on her voice as he watched. Slowly in. Slowly out.

"Oh, Joel, that feels so good. I feel it all the way up my spine. Oh, god, oh, god . . . mmmmm, Joel. Feels—so—good," she whispered in time with his strokes. He felt her fingers working her clit furiously.

"You're telling me," he said breathlessly. His balls tightened. He was so close. Between the tight warmth of her ass and her voice, all he wanted to do was shoot into her. "Gonna come, baby, I'm gonna come!" His voice rose, moans turning into cries. In the distance he heard her call out his name, mixed with "Oh, god!" His cock was suddenly gripped as Jessica's orgasm hit her. Intense pleasure waves rose from his balls, up his shaft, through the tip. He cried out as the first shot of come pulsed into her, followed by another and another. Her ass gripped him like a velvet glove. He felt each wave from base to tip as his cock emptied into her. The last stormy contraction brought him back into his body. He became aware of her tight ass surrounding his cock again, of nerves being brought sharply into focus. The skin at the base of his spine tingled.

He realized his fingers were digging into her waist. He forced his hands to loosen, to slowly stroke her hips as their breathing returned to normal. "Oh, god, that felt good," she said. She took a deep breath. His cock was still firmly inside her. He began to slowly pull out, and Jessica let out a low growl. "Wow," he mumbled, pressing his semihard shaft against her body. He pulled her close, letting his arms circle her waist and his head rest on the back of her shoulder.

"You can say that again," Jessica said. She turned around and faced him, their soapy bodies sliding easily. "See? Evening showers can be so relaxing," she giggled as she reached for Joel's neck, pulled him down, and kissed him soundly. A soap bubble on his cheek popped as he pulled her under the lukewarm spray. "The best part," she said, "is the cleanup!"

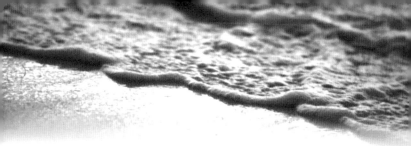

Mer

FRANCESCA LIA BLOCK

SHE RISES UP FROM THE WATER, THE DROPS SLICKING HER breasts, beading tremulous at her nipples. The curve of her hips sheathed tight in something sheer and silver, glimmering beneath the narrow swoon of her waist. She tosses her head and smiles at him; her mouth is like the shadowy place nestled under the fabric that he knows he can never reach. He lumbers across the grasping sand toward the water, his cock leading him, plunging him into the wet salt swell.

When Tom Mac wakes he can still taste the waves and feel his limbs rocking; there is a silver-green light in his head and he has a massive hard-on. He knows there has been more to the dream, but he can't remember, and after a few minutes his erection is gone.

Maybe I'll go out today, he thinks, but he knows he won't surf. It has been too long already. It would only remind him of how it had been before. He gets out of bed to take a piss and sees his reflection in the mirror—sandy-blond longish hair and tan bristly skin, lines around his blue-green eyes. His body has grown thick and slow, the once-taut bulging muscles losing their tone. What would Tawny say if she saw him now? That she was right. Right for leaving. That she could have predicted this—the ex-pro living in the house now overgrown with wisteria vines, drinking too much, hanging out on the boardwalk, never touching his board.

Instead of going back to bed, like usual, he throws on the shirt that smells the least—a hooded woven thing from Mexico, a pair of shorts and huaraches. His heart is thumping as if he really is going back in the water—he knows he isn't. But he also knows he has to get to the pier before the sun and the crowds. He has to get out there.

It is still early and gray and damp. A mist hangs in the air, clings to his hair and skin, tasting of ocean. *Sometimes it was like fucking*, he finds himself thinking—for the first time in so long—*when you rode the waves, feeling them folding around you, glistening and wet and briny.* And he can hardly remember either of them.

The boardwalk is almost empty. Later the vendors will arrive with their crystals and T-shirts and cheap sunglasses; the fortune-tellers and clowns and acrobats will come, the bodybuilders and Rollerbladers and tourists. But now it is just Sage and Whitman and a few of the other homeless whose names no one seems to know, huddled on graffiti-scrawled wooden benches. Even the surfers haven't shown up; the sea looks flat and steely. The cans are brimming with junk-food remnants, pigeons are scavenging; there is a slightly toxic smell. Tom thinks, *And this is paradise, this is my paradise.* Remembering Tawny dancing to the drums right here, that night, with her breasts straining the bikini top and the tie-dyed sarong hanging low under her flat brown stomach. Her hair still crusted with salt, and the way she always smelled like summer.

Tom buys five cups of coffee and distributes four to the men on the bench, keeping one, sipping it even though it is still scalding, liking the feel of the burn on his tongue. Whitman says, "You up early, Mac," and Tom nods. *Had a dream*, he wants to say. They would probably understand. They aren't that much different than he is. Dreams, mostly forgotten, that keep you going when otherwise you might decide not to wake up again. And he is the lucky one, isn't he? Has the house to keep away the cold.

The house he'd bought at the height of things, when he and Tawny first met, when he wanted a base in Southern California to return to between exotic wave-chasings. It is a small white Craftsman bungalow with a glassed-in porch, big windows; the wisteria vine with its purple blossoms has grown so thick now that not much light gets in anymore. Tawny liked the wood floors bare and cool, the rooms mostly empty except for bed and pillows and boards. Now it is cluttered with shit, and he keeps promising himself that he is going to do something about that.

Instead of going back, he walks down the boardwalk with his cup of coffee. He draws up his hood because the mist is forming drops now, but he doesn't want to go home. The dream still whirls in the pit of his stomach, making his muscles twitch, scratching at his balls.

The girl in the wheelchair rides toward him out of the grayness. When he sees her, Tom MacDougal feels as if he has swallowed a mouthful of salt water and it is caught in his throat. There are beautiful babes all the time, everywhere at the beach, but rarely this. So beautiful that he hardly notices the wheelchair or that her legs are wrapped in tight silvery fabric covered with half-moon shaped spangles.

As she approaches him, she smiles as if she knows him. Her teeth are white and sharp and her lips are stung, wet. He just keeps staring. Her eyes are crystally green and wide-spaced. Her breasts show through her soaked T-shirt, every curve and swell and the tender dark nipples, so he feels as if he is touching them. Then she runs her long slender fingers over her collarbone, lingering beneath the slope of her breasts, and pulls the T-shirt off. Rain spills in rivulets over her perfect brown body. *Perfect*, he thinks. *She is perfect.*

Crazy perfect, like him, alone in the rain, pulling off her shirt for a stranger.

He approaches her slowly, the way you would a startled animal, although she doesn't seem afraid. His voice is hoarse and soft. "You okay?"

She nods, still smiling at him. He tries not to stare at her breasts. They seem too big for her delicate frame; her waist is so small and her ribs showing. "You'll get cold, sweetheart."

She shakes her head, swinging the matted blond dreadlocks that hang to her waist.

"Do you need some help?" he asks her.

She gestures for him to come close. He can feel his cock stirring in his shorts. Smelling her; she is clean, salty. He wants to dive. Her nipples are erect; he wants to feel them against his lips. Everything tingling.

She reaches up and touches the side of his unshaven face with her finger, letting it slide down over his Adam's apple. "Take me home with you," she says softly.

The whole impact of the dream is back suddenly; his penis throbbing. He takes off the woven shirt and gives it to her. "Put this on. You'll get sick."

She pouts slightly like a little girl but does it, getting caught so that he has to help her, trying to avoid touching her breasts. Her head emerges through the neck hole of the shirt, those eyes and that sly sweet mouth so close to him, that wild hair. "Take me home, Mac."

He figures one of the guys at the beach has told her his name. But still it startles him. And he wants to know.

Tom wheels the girl back up the boardwalk across the street to the house. He leaves the wheelchair at the foot of the porch and takes her in his arms. She is very light, but longer than she looks in the chair. Her lower body feels much more muscular than he would have thought, the tight weight of her ass against his forearms and wrists. Her slender arms circle his neck the way a child's might. He feels something like power returning to him, like right before he used to take a wave.

"This is a pretty house," she says, staring at the purple blossoms that have grown over everything. "It's like being underwater."

Sometimes I wish it was, he feels like saying. He puts her down gently on the torn couch, then goes to get her chair.

"Do you want to take a bath? I can give you a pair of pants." She laughs and shakes her head. "What about coffee? Or I think there's a can of soup somewhere."

She makes a little face and laughs again. "You look different," she says.

He squints at her. "We've met? I think I'd have remembered you, sweetheart."

"It was a long time ago, Mac." She adds matter-of-factly, "You were unconscious."

Tom sits beside her on the sprung sofa. She plays with her hair, pulling the heavy, knotty strands up off her face. She has very high cheekbones and a small firm chin that makes her lips look even fuller. "What's your name?" Tom asks.

"Mer."

He shakes his head. "Do you want to fill me in here, darling?"

Instead, she smiles again and pulls his shirt off of her. She lifts her hands to her hair again so her breasts rise. The aureoles are big and dark. He wants to hide his hard cock. She takes his tense hands in hers and presses them against her breasts. He feels an electric shock go through him at their breadth and smooth fullness. They feel soft and heavy and almost buzzing with sensation. She throws her head back and moans roughly as he fingers her nipples. Her whole body shudders and she takes his head and gently draws him to her left breast; his tongue circles the nipple and her body is shaking more now. She leans closer to him, pressing her big succulent mouth to his neck. His breath comes in gasps, and his heart pounds as if he is drowning. She moves over his rough, bare, sun-darkened chest with her lips. His cock feels huge, full of ocean.

"Who are you?"

She keeps going, looking up at him sometimes, smiling with those sharp white teeth that could tear; he gently touches the back of her head, the tender nape of her neck, stroking her. Her spine looks fluid and fragile. She undoes his shorts slowly, softly, her nimble fingers sliding the zipper down carefully to avoid his erection. Then he's out, big in her hand. Holding him, she slithers back up and runs her tongue over his mouth, parting his lips with hers, sliding her tongue into him. The salt tastes of his dream. He jolts as her fingers move on his cock. She goes down again, this time her mouth on him, taking him all in one slide so that he feels the back of her throat.

While she licks and sucks, her lips cupping the tender head of his penis and then swallowing him to the balls, Tom is remembering the dream. That time when he had the accident. What really happened. The waves pulling him down. No air. Just this endless shining blue that he didn't really want to leave. He could have stayed there. He could have stayed. But then something was holding him; he knew he was safe. Rocking him like a baby. And her strong slender body carrying him back to the light, to the air. *Because you belong here,* she told him. *I can't keep you. Even though you are the most beautiful of all of them. And you know my ocean more than any of them will ever know it.* Tom moves with her, his groin spasming, his cock driving farther into her wetness. Suddenly there is that feeling in his balls. He doesn't want it yet but it is too much, he feels his whole body waking from some long sleep, as if he has been underwater this whole time and only now has she rescued him. He gasps for air as he breaks through the surface, his semen spurting out in milky bursts that she swallows, his cock still hard for a long time after, still coming into her lush mouth.

Mer stays with Tom MacDougal in the little beach house with the wisteria wine and the glass porch. No one knows what goes on in there, only that Mac has started surfing again, every day, up at dawn with the kids, taking the big waves, ferocious and fearless as he had been ten years ago. And that his mysterious young girlfriend in the wheelchair sits on the sand and watches him. When he returns from the sea, he plunges to his knees before her and kisses her as if she contains the breath he had lost that time he almost drowned. Maybe she does. People speculate as to how they fuck, what is under the narrow spangled sheath she always wears over her lower body. Some think she is crazy, playing out some fantasy so he can't get inside her. Maybe she'd been molested as a child or raped as a teenager, traveling along the coast, and that's why she invented the wheelchair thing and the costume. Others think it is real. But Mac and Mer don't care. His mouth on her tender, swollen, glossy breasts, making her come when he caresses her nipples; her mouth sliding down the shaft of his thick cock, they rescue each other from land and from sea again and again.

Naked Woman Playing Chopin
A Fargo Romance

LOUISE ERDRICH

THE STREET THAT RUNS ALONG THE RED RIVER FOLLOWS THE curves of a stream that is muddy and shallow, full of brush, silt, and oxbows that throw the whole town off the strict clean grid laid out by railroad plat. The river floods most springs and drags local back-yards into its flow, even though its banks are strengthened with riprap and piled high with concrete torn from reconstructed streets and basements. It is a hopelessly complicated river, one that freezes deceptively, breaks rough, drowns one or two every year in its icy flow. It is a dead river in some places, one that harbors only carp and bullheads. Wild in others, it lures moose down from Canada into the city limits. At one time, when the land along its banks was newly broken, paddleboats and barges of grain moved grandly from its source to Winnipeg, for the river flows inscrutably north. And, over on the Minnesota side, across from what is now church land and the town park, a farm spread generously up and down the river and back into wide hot fields.

The bonanza farm belonged to Easterners who had sold a foundry in Vermont and with their money bought the flat vastness that lay along the river. They raised astounding crops when the land was young—rutabagas that weighed sixty pounds, wheat unbearably lush, corn on cobs like truncheons. Then there were six grasshopper years during which even the handles on the hoes and rakes were eaten and a cavalry soldier, too, was partially devoured while he lay drunk in the insects' path. The enterprise suffered losses on a grand scale. The farm was split among four brothers, eventually, who then sold off half of each so that, by the time Berndt Vogel escaped the trench war of Europe where he'd been chopped mightily but inconclusively in six places by a British cavalry sabre and then kicked by a horse so that his jaw never shut right again, there was just one beautiful and peaceful swatch of land about to go for grabs. In the time it took him to gather—by forswearing women, drinking low beers only, and working twenty-hour days—the money to retrieve the farm from the local bank, its price had dropped further and further, as the earth rose up in a great ship of destruction. Sails of dust carried half of Berndt's lush dirt over the horizon, but enough remained for him to plant and reap six fields.

So Berndt survived. On his land there stood an old hangar-like barn, with only one small part still in use—housing a cow, chickens, one depressed pig. Berndt kept the rest in decent repair, not only because as a good German he must waste nothing that came his way, but also because he saw in those grand, dust-filled shafts of light something that he could worship. It had once housed teams of great blue Percherons and Belgian draft horses. Only one horse was left, old and made of brutal velvet, but the others still moved in the powerful synchronicity of his dreams. He fussed over the remaining mammoth and imagined his farm one day entire, vast and teeming, crews of men under his command, a cookhouse, a bunkhouse, equipment, a woman and children sturdily determined to their toil, and a garden in which seeds bearing the scented pinks and sharp red geraniums of his childhood were planted and thrived.

How surprised he was to find, one afternoon, as though sown by the wind and summoned by his dreams, a woman standing barefoot, starved and frowsy in the doorway of his barn. She was a pale flower, nearly bald and dressed in a rough shift. He blinked stupidly at the vision. Light poured around her like smoke and swirled at her gesture of need. She spoke.

"*Ich habe Hunger.*"

By the way she said it, he knew she was a Swabian and therefore—he tried to thrust the thought from his mind—liable to have certain unruly habits in bed. He passed his hand across his eyes. Through the gown of nearly transparent muslin he could see that her breasts were, excitingly, bound tightly to her chest with strips of cloth. He blinked hard. Looking directly into her eyes, he experienced the vertigo of confronting a female who did not blush or look away but held him with an honest human calm. He thought at first that she must be a loose woman, fleeing a brothel—had Fargo got so big? Or escaping an evil marriage, perhaps. He didn't know she was from God.

In the center of the town on the other side of the river there stood a convent made of yellow bricks. Hauled halfway across Minnesota from Little Falls by pious drivers, they still held the peculiar sulfurous moth gold of the clay outside that town. The word "Fleisch" was etched in shallow letters on each one: Fleisch Company Brickworks. Donated to the nuns at cost. The word, of course, was covered by mortar each time a brick was laid. However, because she had organized a few discarded bricks behind the convent into the base for a small birdbath, one of the younger nuns knew, as she gazed at the mute order of the convent's wall, that she lived within the secret repetition of that one word.

She had once been Agnes DeWitt and now was Sister Cecellia, shorn, houseled, clothed in black wool and bound in starched linen of heatless white. She not only taught but lived music, existed for those hours when she could be concentrated in her being—which was half music, half divine light, flesh only to the degree that she could not admit otherwise. At the piano keyboard, absorbed into the notes that rose beneath her hands, she existed in her essence, a manifestation of compelling sound. Her hands were long and thick-veined, very white, startling against her habit. She rubbed them with lard and beeswax nightly to keep them supple. During the day, when she graded papers or used the blackboard her hands twitched and drummed, patterned and repatterned difficult fingerings. She was no trouble to live with and her obedience was absolute. Only, and with increasing concentration, she played Brahms, Beethoven, Debussy, Schubert, and Chopin.

It wasn't that she neglected her other duties; rather, it was the playing itself—distilled of longing—that disturbed her sisters. In her music Sister Cecellia explored profound emotions. She spoke of her faith and doubt, of her passion as the bride of Christ, of her loneliness, shame, ultimate redemption. The Brahms she played was thoughtful, the Schubert confounding. Debussy was all contrived nature and yet as gorgeous as a meadowlark. Beethoven contained all messages, but her crescendos lacked conviction. When it came to Chopin, however, she did not use the flowery ornamentation or the endless trills and insipid floribunda of so many of her day. Her playing was of the utmost sincerity. And Chopin, played simply, devastates the heart. Sometimes a pause between the piercing sorrows of minor notes made a sister scrubbing the floor weep into the bucket where she dipped her rag so that the convent's boards, washed in tears, seemed to creak in a human tongue. The air of the house thickened with sighs.

Sister Cecellia, however, was emptied. Thinned. It was as though her soul were neatly removed by a drinking straw and siphoned into the green pool of quiet that lay beneath the rippling cascades of notes. One day, exquisite agony built and released, built higher, released more forcefully until slow heat spread between her fingers, up her arms, stung at the points of her bound breasts, and then shot straight down.

Her hands flew off the keyboard— she crouched as though she had been shot, saw yellow spots, and experienced a peaceful wave of oneness in which she entered pure communion. She was locked into the music, held there safely, entirely understood. Such was her innocence that she didn't know she was experiencing a sexual climax, but believed, rather, that what she felt was the natural outcome of this particular nocturne played to the utmost of her skills—and so it came to be. Chopin's spirit became her lover. His flats caressed her. His whole notes sank through her body like clear pebbles. His atmospheric trills were the flicker of a tongue. His pauses before the downward sweep of notes nearly drove her insane.

The Mother Superior knew something had to be done when she herself woke, her face bathed in sweat and tears, to the insinuating soft largo of the Prelude in E Minor. In those notes she remembered the death of her mother and sank into an endless afternoon of her loss. The Mother Superior then grew, in her heart, a weed of rage against the God who had taken a mother from a seven-year-old child whose world she was, entirely, without question—heart, arms, guidance, soul—until by evening she felt fury steaming from the hot marrow of her bones and stopped herself.

"Oh, God, forgive me," the Superior prayed. She considered humunculation, but then rushed down to the piano room instead, and with all of the strength in her wide old arms gathered and hid from Cecellia every piece of music but the Bach.

After that, for some weeks, there was relief. Sister Cecellia turned to the Two-Part Inventions. Her fingers moved on the keys with the precision of an insect building its nest. She played each as though she were constructing an airtight box. Stealthily, once Cecellia had moved on to Bach's other works, the Mother Superior removed from the music cabinet and destroyed the Goldberg Variations—clearly capable of lifting subterranean complexities into the mind. Life in the convent returned to normal. The cook, to everyone's gratitude, stopped preparing the rancid, goose-fat-laced beet soup of her youth and stuck to overcooked string beans, cabbage, potatoes. The floors stopped groaning and absorbed fresh wax. The doors ceased to fly open for no reason and closed discreetly. The water stopped rushing through the pipes as the sisters no longer took continual advantage of the new plumbing to drown out the sounds of their emotions.

And then one day Sister Cecellia woke with a tightness in her chest. Pain shot through her and the red lump in her rib cage beat like a wild thing caught in a snare of bones. Her throat shut. She wept. Her hands, drawn to the keyboard, floated into a long appoggiatura. Then, crash, she was inside a thrusting mazurka. The music came back to her. There was the scent of faint gardenias—his hothouse boutonnière. The silk of his heavy brown hair. His sensuous drawing-room sweat. His voice—she heard it—avid and light. It was as if the composer himself had entered the room. Who knows? Surely there was no more desperate, earthly, exacting heart than Cecellia's. Surely something, however paltry, lies beyond the grave.

At any rate, she played Chopin. Played him in utter naturalness until the Mother Superior was forced to shut the cover to the keyboard and gently pull the stool away. Cecellia lifted the lid and played upon her knees. The poor scandalized dame dragged her from the keys. Cecellia crawled back. The Mother, at her wit's end, sank down and urged the young woman to pray. She herself spoke first in fear and then in certainty, saying that it was the very Devil who had managed to find a way to Cecellia's soul through the flashing doors of sixteenth notes. Her fears were confirmed when, not moments later, the gentle sister raised her arms and fists and struck the keys as though the instrument were stone and from the rock her thirst would be quenched. But only discord emerged.

"My child, my dear child," the Mother comforted, "come away and rest yourself."

The younger nun, breathing deeply, refused. Her severe gray eyes were rimmed in a smoky red. Her lips bled purple. She was in torment. "There is no rest," she declared. She unpinned her veil and studiously dismantled her habit, folding each piece with reverence and setting it upon the piano bench. The Mother remonstrated with Cecellia in the most tender and compassionate tones. However, just as in the depth of her playing the virgin had become the woman, so now the woman in the habit became a woman to the bone. She stripped down to her shift, but no further.

"He wouldn't want me to go out unprotected," she told her Mother Superior.

"God?" the older woman asked, bewildered.

"Chopin," Cecellia answered.

Kissing her dear Mother's trembling fingers, Cecellia knelt. She made a true genuflection, murmured an act of contrition, and then walked away from the convent made of bricks with the secret word pressed between yellow mortar, and from the music, her music, which the Mother Superior would from then on keep under lock and key.

So it was Sister Cecellia, or Agnes DeWitt of rural Wisconsin, who appeared before Berndt Vogel in the cavern of the barn and said in her mother's dialect, for she knew a German when she met one, that she was hungry. She wanted to ask whether he had a piano, but it was clear to her that he wouldn't and at any rate she was exhausted.

"*Jetzt muss ich schlafen*," she said after eating half a plate of scalded oatmeal with new milk.

So he took her to his bed, the only bed there was, in the corner of the otherwise empty room. He went out to the barn he loved, covered himself with hay, and lay awake all night listening to the rustling of mice and sensing the soundless predatory glide of the barn owls and the stiff erratic flutter of bats. By morning, he had determined to marry her if she would have him, just so that he could unpin and then unwind the long strip of cloth that bound her torso. She refused his offer, but she did speak to him of who she was and where from, and in that first summary she gave of her life she concluded that she must never marry again, for not only had she wed

herself soul to soul to Christ, but she had already been unfaithful—
with her phantom lover, the Polish composer. She had already lived
out too grievous a destiny to become a bride again. By explaining this
to Berndt, however, she had merely moved her first pawn in a long
game of words and gestures that the two would play over the course
of many months. What she didn't know was that she had opened to
a dogged and ruthless opponent.

Berndt Vogel's passion engaged him, mind and heart. He prepared
himself. Having dragged Army caissons through hip-deep mud after
the horses died in torment, having seen his best friend suddenly
uncreated into a mass of shrieking pulp, having lived intimately with
pouring tumults of eager lice and rats plump with horrifying food, he
was rudimentarily prepared for the suffering he would experience in
love. She, however, had also learned her share of discipline.
Moreover—for the heart of her gender is stretched, pounded, molded,
and tempered for its hot task from birth—she was a woman.

The two struck a temporary bargain, and set up
housekeeping. She still slept in the indoor bed. He stayed in the
barn. A month passed. Three. Six. Each morning she lit the stove
and cooked, then heated water in a big tank for laundry and swept
the cool linoleum floors. Monday she sewed. She baked all day
Tuesday. On Wednesdays she churned and scrubbed. She sold the
butter and the eggs Thursdays. Killed a chicken every Friday.
Saturdays she walked into town and practiced piano in the school
basement. Sunday she played the organ for Mass and then at the
close of the day started the next week's work. Berndt paid her. At
first she spent her salary on clothing. When with her earnings she
had acquired shoes, stockings, a full set of cotton underclothing and
then a woolen one, too, and material for two housedresses—one
patterned with twisted leaves and tiny blue berries, and the other of
an ivy lattice print—and a sweater and, at last, a winter coat, after
she had earned a blanket, quilted overalls, a pair of boots, she
decided on a piano.

This is where Berndt thought he could maneuver her into marriage, but she proved too cunning for him. It was early in the evening and the yard was pleasant with the sound of grasshoppers. The two sat on the porch drinking glasses of sugared lemon water. Every so often, in the ancient six-foot grasses that survived at the margin of the yard, a firefly signaled or a dove cried out its five hollow notes.

They drank slowly, she in her sprigged-berry dress that skimmed her waist. He noted with disappointment that she wore normal underclothing now, had stopped binding her breasts. Perhaps, he thought, he could persuade her to resume her old ways, at least occasionally, just for him. It was a wan hope. She looked so comfortable, so free. She'd taken on a little weight and lost her anemic pallor. Her arms were brown, muscular. In the sun, her straight fine hair glinted with green-gold sparks of light and her eyes were deceptively clear.

"I can teach music," she told him. She had decided that her suggestion must sound merely practical, a money-making ploy. She did not express any pleasure or zeal, though at the very thought each separate tiny muscle in her hands ached. "It would be a way of bringing in some money."

He was left to absorb this. He might have believed her casual proposition, except that her restless fingers gave her away, and he noted their insistent motions. She was playing the Adagio of the "Pathétique" on the tablecloth, a childhood piece that nervously possessed her from time to time.

"You would need a piano," he told her. She nodded and held his gaze in that aloof and unbearably sexual way that had first skewered him.

"It's the sort of thing a husband gives his wife," he dared.

Her fingers stopped moving. She cast down her eyes in contempt.

"I can use the school instrument. I've spoken to the school principal already."

Berndt looked at the moon-shaped bone of her ankle, at her foot in the brown, thick-heeled shoe she'd bought. He ached to hold her foot in his lap, untie her oxford shoe with his teeth, cover her calf with kisses, and breathe against the delicate folds of berry cloth.

He offered marriage once again. His heart. His troth. His farm. She spurned the lot. She would simply walk into town. He let her know that he would like to buy the piano, it wasn't that, but there was not a store for many miles where it could be purchased. She knew better and with exasperated heat described the way that she would, if he would help financially, go about locating and then acquiring the best piano for the best price. She vowed that she would purchase the instrument not in Fargo but in Minneapolis. From there, she could have it hauled for less than the freight markup. She would make her arrangements in one day and return by night in order not to spend one extra dime either on food she couldn't carry or on a hotel room. When he resisted to the last, she told him that she was leaving. She would find a small room in town and there she would acquire students, give lessons.

She betrayed her desperation. Some clench of her fingers gave her away, and it was as much Berndt's unconfused love of her and wish that she might be happy as any worry she might leave him that finally caused him to agree. In the six months that he'd known Agnes DeWitt she had become someone to reckon with, and even he, who understood desperation and self-denial, was finding her proximity most difficult. He worked himself into exhaustion, and his farm prospered. Sleeping in the barn was difficult, but he had set into one wall a bunk room for himself and his hired man and installed a stove that burned red hot on cold nights; only, sometimes, as he looked sleepily into the glowering flanks of iron, he could not keep his own fingers from moving along the rough mattress in faint imitation of the way he would, if he ever could, touch her hips. He, too, was practicing.

drunk on the unlikely eagerness of the other's body. These frenzied periods occurred every so often, like spells in the weather. They would be drawn, sink, disappear into their greed, until the cow groaned for milking or the hired man swore and banged on the outside gate. If nothing else intervened, they'd stop from sheer exhaustion. Then they would look at one another oddly, questingly, as if the other person were a complete stranger, and gradually resume their normal interaction, which was offhand and distracted, but upheld by the assurance of people who thought alike.

Agnes gave music lessons, and although the two weren't married, even the Catholics and the children came to her. This was because it was well-known that Miss DeWitt's first commitment had been to Christ. It was understandable that she would have no other marriage. Although she did not take the Holy Eucharist on her tongue, she was there at church each Sunday morning, faithful and devout, to play the organ. There, she, of course, played Bach, with a purity of intent purged of any subterranean feeling, strictly, and for God.

So when the river began to rise one spring, Berndt had already gone where life was deepest many times, and he did not particularly fear the rain. But what began as a sheer mist became an even sprinkle and then developed into a slow, pounding shower that lasted three days, then four, then on the fifth day, increased.

The river boiled along swiftly, a gray soup still contained, just barely, within its high banks. On day six the rain stopped, or seemed to. The storm had moved upstream. All day while the sun shone pleasantly the river heaved itself up, tore into its flow new trees and boulders, created tip-ups, washouts, areas of singing turbulence, and crawled, like an infant, toward the farm. Berndt rushed around uneasily, pitching hay into the high loft, throwing chickens up after the hay, wishing he could throw the horse up as well, and the house, and—because Agnes wrung her hands—the piano. But the piano was earth-anchored and well-tuned by the rainy air, so, instead of worrying, Agnes practiced.

Once the river started to move, it gained confidence. It had no problem with fences or gates, wispy windbreaks, ditches. It simply leveled or attained the level of whatever stood in its path. Water jumped up the lawn and collected behind the sacks of sand that Berndt had desperately filled and laid. The river tugged itself up the porch and into the house from one side. From the other side it undermined an already weak foundation that had temporarily shored up the same wall once removed to make way for the piano. The river tore against the house and then, like a child tipping out a piece of candy from a box, it surged underneath and rocked the floor, and the piano crashed through the weakened wall.

It landed in the swift current of the yard, Agnes with it. Berndt saw only the white treble clef of her dress as she spun away, clutching the curved lid. It bobbed along the flower beds first, and then, as muscular new eddies caught it, touched down on the shifting lanes of Berndt's wheat fields, and farther, until the revolving instrument and the woman on it reached the original river and plunged in. They were carried not more than a hundred feet before the piano lost momentum and sank. As it went down, Agnes thought at first of crawling into its box, nestling for safety among the cold, dead strings. But, as she struggled with the hinged cover, she lost her grip and was swept north. She should have drowned, but there was a snag of rope, a tree, two men in a fishing skiff risking themselves to save a valuable birding dog. They pulled Agnes out and dumped her in the bottom of the boat, impatient to get the dog. She gagged, coughed, and passed out in a roil of feet and fishing tackle.

When she came to, she was back in the convent, which was on high ground and open to care for victims of the flood. Berndt was not among the rescued. When the river went down and the heat rose, he was found snagged in a tip-up of roots, tethered to his great blue steaming horse. As Agnes recovered her strength, did she dream of him? Think of him entering her and her receiving him? Long for the curve of his hand on her breast? Yes and no. She thought again of music. Chopin. Berndt. Chopin.

He had written a will, in which he declared her his common-law wife and left to her the farm and all upon it. There, she raised Rosecomb Bantams, Dominikers, Reds. She bought another piano and played with an isolated intensity that absorbed her spirit.

A year or so after Berndt's death, her students noticed that she would stop in the middle of a lesson and smile out the window as though welcoming a long-expected visitor. One day the neighbor children went to pick up the usual order of eggs and were most struck to see the white-and-black-flecked Dominikers flapping up in alarm around Miss DeWitt as she stood magnificent upon the green grass.

Tall, slender, legs slightly bowed, breasts jutting a bit to either side, and the flare of hair flicking up the center of her—naked. She looked at the children with remote kindness. Asked, "How many dozen?" Walked off to gather the eggs.

That episode made the gossip-table rounds. People put it off to Berndt's death and a relapse of nerves. She lost only a Lutheran student or two. She continued playing the organ for the Mass, and at home, in the black, black nights, Chopin. And if she was asked, by an innocent pupil too young to understand the meaning of discretion, why she sometimes didn't wear clothes, Miss DeWitt would answer that she removed her clothing when she played the music of a particular bare-souled composer. She would nod meditatively and say in her firmest manner that when one enters into such music, one should be naked. And then she would touch the keys.

Gliuccioni and the River God

HEATHER CORINNA

IN THE BEGINNING, YOU WERE SIMPLY GOOD AT WHAT YOU DID, and better than most.

No one cared, aside of the occasional whistle, sleight of hand under slide of ass, and when you delivered the goods—quicker, faster, cleaner than any of the mongrels who tried to best you—no one dared insist you were anything but the best. Even if you were a dame; even while they cheated you for your due.

But he noticed, and from the start, you knew that when that happened, it was only going to go one way or another: your way or his. Someone good can run the docks, but you'd have to be a fucking fountain in Sicily to beat the river god on his turf.

"Arethusa Gliuccioni," he announced. You'd turned quickly, hand too fast to the piece. The adrenaline from the job was still rushing through sinew and muscle; you were jumpy as a rookie.

"Mr. Alpheus," you'd said, seeing him, taking in a few quick breaths to calm yourself, sliding the weapon back in your boot. "Beg pardon, sir, this time of night, on the docks, I didn't—"

He waved you off. "No need," he said, and grinned like the cat who'd eaten more than one canary in his day. And he had. "You finished?"

You wiped your brow, shook the water from your hands. "Yeah, he's done. Sank like a stone. You want this now, or—" You shook the grocery bag in his direction, heartbeat in your throat from the fear and the rush.

"No, no," he spoke with a smile. "You keep it this time. That's not so easy for a dame to do, no?"

"It's easy enough for me, and probably for him, in the long run. Faster anyway, less painful. I'll get paid for the job in time, this is yours."

He shook his head again. "Not this time. You keep it all. I'll tell the boys we're all settled up. You hungry?"

You shouldn't have, but, not one to be bested, not one to turn down the dare, you went to dinner anyway; sopped up green olive oil with bread where you sat alone in the back of the restaurant, and listened instead of talking. You had to listen, there was no way around it, it was how the game was played if you wanted to win.

You had to say yes when he asked if you'd like to go to your place, and you had to go with it when he curled his finger under your chin and brought your lips up to his, breath thick with wine and cigar smoke, and you had to kiss him like you meant it, like your life depended on it. And it did.

The story didn't have to go this way, though; you could say good night and let it go at that and keep on with your job, except that you were too good at it, and had close to a hundred grand lined up in neat little rows right under the mattress you sat on with him, and another batch still to go back and get from tonight's job, like you always did. With your lips on his, you had to wonder if what you smelled was wine or suspicion.

You can't be too careful when you're this slippery, so instead of saying good night, you got on your knees and ran your fingernails over that perfectly ironed white silk shirt, making his dark nipples rise up as you undid his belt with your teeth and let him unbutton and unzip himself so you didn't seem too bossy. You knew you might be okay then, and so you let him hold his cock to your mouth and run the slick tip of it in circles over your lips, and you slid your hot tongue back and forth and back again underneath it, fingertips slipping around his balls, stroking their fur like the head of a cat.

Once you heard him start to groan and call your name, you knew you were home free. You got off on the blowjob, knowing you were sucking the boss right on top of every dollar you deserved for your work but never got and so you stole. Isn't it ironic, considering the fucking bag you offered him was empty, and that irony, and the feeling of getting away with it, and that goddamn smell of money and sweat got you wet. It was a damn good thing your mouth was full, it kept you from laughing your head off. You pulled your mouth up and down over his purpling dick, and his hands pulled at your ears hungry and needy as you sucked it hard against the roof of your mouth, milking the fleshy cow. It spat out praise in a bitter, milky shot that you slammed down your throat with an audible sigh, then you smiled, wiped your lips on the back of your hand.

He looked at you after, not warmly, but with a little special what-the-hell-is-it-for-chrissakes something you couldn't place.

"Arethusa Gliuccioni," he said, pulling a handful of bills from under the mattress. "You belong to me."

He came for you the next day, after you spent a day pacing and planning and fucking praying to whomever would hear for this to go right. You knew it would happen; it had to, and you didn't dare try and run out and end up less nine fingers or toes, or with half a leg or one eye to show for it, only to die later anyway.

The rope ate at your ankles, tight against the legs of the chair. There you were, on the dock's edge, where you'd taken the others before; the tables turned. He sat across in his own chair, looking smug, waiting for the help, never one to get blood on his own manicured hands. He hadn't even bothered tying down your hands—why would he bother? What could you do to him, without even a gun?

He shook his head back and forth like a slow metronome. "Things could have been easy for you, chickie, with that pretty face, and that soft mouth, and everything else you've got in that nice package of yours. You were good, too. A man would be hard-pressed to find another dame that could deliver like that in bed and on the dock."

You sat in silence; mind alert like a hawk, taking it all in, measuring every detail and comparing every possibility. Somehow, though, you knew, even when it looked that bad, the water behind you chilly as you knew it was, air on the dock reeking of dead fish, you knew which way it'd go. One way or another.

"You have anything to say to me, Gliuccioni?" he asked.

You knew what to say as much as you knew that water below. "I'll give it all back, Mr. Alpheus. You know I will, and I'll do anything for you you want. If I had known before last night—"

"You had a good time last night?"

"You know I did."

"That's a shame. And you've done good work for me. I can't say you haven't, even with you skimming the whole time. And last night"—he paused, smiling softly to himself—"You did good then too." He sighed.

"But it's too late for that, isn't it?"

You slid your legs open slowly, as much as you could with the ropes on your ankles, as much as you could without him catching on, but enough for him to get where it could go; where he thought it could go.

He smiled again, cruelly. "You trying to show me what I missed? Not a whole lot we can do, you stuck to that chair like that, and I'd be a fool to put my dick in your mouth when you're about to say good-bye. Especially when I still don't know where the money that was supposed to be in that bag last night went."

You looked at him with your dark eyes and full mouth and opened your legs some more, cursing your beauty for getting you into this, and fucking praying it would get you out. And it would. You knew that much, and maybe he knew it too.

He sat down on his chair across from you. "All right, chickie. Show me, then you talk," he said.

And you did. There was no way he couldn't watch as you slipped your fingers over your cunt and slid the lips open so he could see the pink there, wet already because you felt your freedom swimming back to you in every second he stayed in that chair across from you and the dock stayed empty. There was no way he could stop looking as you wet your fingers in that hole and pulled them out, sticky, to roll them over your clit slowly, your eyes glued to his face.

Over the smell of rotten fish, fear, and power, you could smell the getaway so close it burned the back of your throat like whiskey. You rubbed yourself a little faster, a little harder, all the while pleading with him for forgiveness. The sound of the water clapping against the rotting wood sung your praises like a choir, and made murky promises you intended to hold it to.

"Show me more, baby," he said, "and maybe we can work something out."

Oh, we can, you thought as you plunged wet fingers deep inside your cunt and flicked the others over your hard clit again and again. The icy air pierced your thighs, and someone's moment of weakness, and someone's advantage was so close. A balance of power hung there, still as stone as he watched you make yourself come under his gaze, chair teetering on the dock's edge, and you moaned loudly, and just as you did, saw that moment and made it yours. And it was.

You threw yourself backward in the chair hard and fast, and he never saw it coming. The wood pulled you down slowly like you knew it would, and you heard him shout, saw his face uncertain but cruel as he watched you slide lower, and thanks to Charlie, your prayers were answered.

Just where you left him last night, where you'd left them all before you could get back in and get your prize, he sat in his own chair, face bloated like a pufferfish, but the briefcase was still in his hand and you knew his piece was right inside, nice and dry in that good Roman leather, just like they always were.

You stuffed the bills from the case as best you could into your coat pockets, letting one, two, three packs float up until you heard the shout. It takes only a second to cut the rope with one of the rocks down here, just like you knew it would. How sad that none of the floaters never even tried.

The story didn't have to end this way—but honey, was it worth it—only one good kick up, and only one shot to set him down in with you forever. You watched him fall, your head light from a quick gulp of air, thighs slick with that juice from moments before, and slicker still with the sure thing of your freedom and winning the game.

You were simply good at what you did, and better than most, and you shot out and swam like a goddamn fountain in Sicily, feeling the story had ended just as you knew it would; as it should.

And it did.

Author's note: According to a traditional Greek myth, Arethusa, sworn to the goddess Artemis, was pursued in lust by the river god, Alpheus. Determined to stay a sacred maiden and independent hunter, Arethusa prayed to her goddess for help. Artemis arrived and carried her to Sicily, where she changed the maiden into a living fountain. Alpheus followed her under the sea and joined his waters with the fountain. It remains known as the Fountain of Arethusa in Syracuse, on the island of Sicily in Italy.

Josie's Rainy Day Man

MARCY SHEINER

DAN STOOD NAKED BEFORE THE FULL-LENGTH MIRROR OF HIS sliding-door closet. Was it his imagination, or had he gotten taller? Thirty-eight-year-old men did not grow taller—he must be standing more erect. He peered closely at his face, noting what appeared to be new wrinkles around his hazel eyes. He didn't mind them, actually, didn't mind having sprouted signs of age. He'd felt like a boy for so long.

It was Josie, he knew, who had changed him. These last three months with her had straightened his back, wrinkled his eyes. And these were only outward changes; he felt different inwardly as well. More sure of himself. More grown up. Like a man.

Josie had unleashed some raw animal hunger he hadn't even known was in him. A virgin way beyond the median age for an American male—twenty-four and two months, to be exact—his sexual experience had until now consisted of three rather short-term relationships prior to a ten-year marriage. He'd thought that he and his wife had had a good sexual relationship—they both got hot, they both got wet, they both came—but now, in light of his newfound wisdom, he regarded it as mere child's play.

There'd been a few women since his divorce with whom Dan had always been the perfect gentleman, in and out of bed. Literally: a gentle man, he never pushed himself on women. He knew the rules of the nineties, considered himself a feminist, believed that loving, sensual, gentle sex was the way it "should" be. And the women, most of them younger than he, had seemed to feel the same.

Nothing in his experience had prepared him for Josie.

Josie, fifty-two, knew what she wanted, when she wanted it, and with whom. Josie, with her almost violent libido, had reached inside his soul and pulled out feelings and needs that almost frightened him in their intensity. At first it had just been dirty talk: "Fuck me, fuck me hard," stuff like that. He'd been mildly shocked; his wife had never talked in bed except to say "I love you." Gradually, Josie's words had evolved into whispered fantasies, wildly elaborate scenarios in which the central theme was his ownership of her. She would arch her neck and pull his lips down to suck, urging, "Harder, harder," until he left dark purple marks that she seemed to prize.

Afterward she'd cuddle up to him like a pet, stroke the hair on his arms, coo like a contented little bird. His heart filled with painful tenderness. The more brutal the lovemaking, the more tender the afterglow.

In bed he owned her; out of bed they were equals. No, that wasn't true: she was certainly more equal than he in this relationship. Not that she exerted power over him in any way—it was just that he felt like a grateful little puppy dog around her, afraid if he did or said the wrong thing she'd end this miraculous sexual journey he wanted so much to continue. What was it someone had said about older women? *They're so grateful.* But he was the one who, outside of bed at least, treated her with solicitous gratitude.

His hand reached down almost reflexively to stroke his cock. Even that seemed to have grown in these past few months, as if in response to her vast need. He was becoming the man Josie needed.

He dressed carefully, in freshly washed jeans and a black T-shirt that showed his muscular, hairy arms. She said she loved his arms, was constantly praising their beauty. Sitting beside him on her tiny sofa, or lying next to him in bed, she would run her hands up and down his arms, stroking them as lovingly as she stroked his cock.

"Rainy Day Man," she called him. "Dan, Dan, my Rainy Day Man," she sang, almost mockingly. When he asked her what it meant, she put on an old, scratched Bonnie Raitt record. A Rainy Day Man, she explained, accepted without judgment a woman's blues.

Josie got the blues a lot. She'd hinted at a dark history that still haunted her. But for Josie, the blues were a motivating factor in sex, as valid as love or celebration. Frequently she cried before, during, or after orgasm. At first he'd been afraid, thought he'd done something wrong, but she assured him that she liked the release.

Josie sat on the front deck of her houseboat, watching the sun go down, smoking the remaining stub of a joint. One or two hits in the evening, that's all she did now. The breeze tugged at the rubber band binding her silver hair, and she undid it, shaking her head to let the wind work its way through her long, straight mane.

Dan would be here soon.

Halfheartedly she considered changing her clothes. She was wearing a pair of paint-splattered jeans, a baggy gray V-neck sweater, and a pair of thong sandals. She ought to go put on something sexy, the black lingerie she bought but never wore. But Dan didn't seem to care what she wore. She liked that, liked not having to do something special for him. The women in the pornographic books she read made elaborate preparations before sex dates. What a bother. She skipped those sections always, went straight for the suck-and-fuck, her vibrator between her legs, going for the quick come, the release that would send her back to work.

Josie created greeting cards. Not sentimental drivel for Hallmark, but fantastic artwork accompanied by profound or funny lines culled from writers, musicians, artists; sometimes she even wrote her own short poems. What had begun as a hobby for friends had turned into a cottage industry (she refused to call it a career). Now she was working on what she called her "Rainy Day" series, inspired by Dan's appearance in her life. Some days, like today, she worked like fire, her hands barely able to keep pace with her brain. Other days nothing came. On those days, Josie thought about her long-dead lover, or her damaged children, or about people in Croatia, Rwanda, right next door in Oakland, until, half mad with grief, she dosed herself with tranquilizers and crawled under the covers. More than once Dan had found her that way.

At first he'd tried to jolly her out of her "depression," as he called it. It took a while for her to make him understand that she would not be jollied, that the only thing he could do was climb under the damn covers and fuck her brains out. If she cried, she cried. Her cunt opened regardless of her mood, her body secreted fluids, she responded even more enthusiastically than on her so-called good days. And so, eventually, he learned to let her be. He didn't really understand it, she knew, but he let her be, and he fucked her.

God, how he fucked her. She'd never known a man so purely and simply *hungry*. At first he'd been gentle, shy, approaching her like a cat lapping its first taste of sweet cream after a lifetime of skim milk. The more she opened to him, though, the bolder he'd become. Now he pawed at her breasts, taking them into his mouth like a starving man. He drank her cunt juice like he needed it for sustenance.

Josie loved the surrender of it. Now that he'd gotten past his tentativeness, she could lie back and give him what she had known he needed. He drank from her breasts, from her cunt: he *took*. But this taking was circular: in responding to Josie's need, Dan was becoming stronger, and in giving him all she had, she got more and more from him. Still, she clung to an idea of herself as his property, her body the territory on which he enacted his deepest desires. This kind of dynamic had always formed the core of Josie's erotic life, and she'd long ago given up feeling diminished by it, or fighting against it.

Dan parked his car by the docks of the Berkeley Marina and got out. The sun had just slipped below the horizon; he spotted Josie's silver hair through the fading light. His cock stirred. He no longer asked if she would be in a good mood, if she would babble on with stories of her trip into town or her encounter with a fisherman— minor incidents she turned into major melodramas with colorful language and theatrical gestures. Or would she be morose, silently leading him to bed without so much as a preliminary kiss on the cheek? It didn't matter. Whatever her mood, the sex was fantastic, soul-moving, creating an intimacy deeper than he'd known even in a decade of daily living with his wife. He walked down the pier, used the key she'd given him to unlock the gate, and climbed up to sit beside her on the boat.

She didn't look up, just reached out and tousled his hair. "Rainy Day Dan," she said softly.

"Is it a rainy day?" he asked.

"Nope. But I'm glad to see you anyway." She turned to kiss him on the lips, clearly a quick hello, but Dan couldn't stop himself from pulling her closer, opening her lips with his tongue.

She sank into him immediately, opening her mouth to allow his tongue to probe inside. It was the same way he probed her cunt, as if searching for something, digging. Dan didn't put only his cock inside her: he also used his tongue, his fingers, his hands. Finger-fucking was the first real sex Josie had ever had, back in her teens, and she'd wished more men engaged in it. That Dan loved to explore her cunt with his hands as much as with his cock was one of his greatest attributes as a lover.

Soon they were lying back on the boat, he moving on top of her, running his hands over her breasts and hips. As sexually adventurous as Josie was, she did not like making love in uncomfortable places, and she pushed him gently off her, stood and took his hand. He followed, puppy-like, down the steps, through the kitchen, down more steps, into her cave of a sleeping alcove where pillows and blankets were piled high.

They stripped quickly, shivering in the damp night air, and climbed into bed. He was on her immediately, spreading her legs, teasing her opening with his stiff cock. She moaned, preparing to surrender.

He would not fuck her right away, she knew. He would first explore that tiny square inch between her legs, drawing out her fluids until she came, and then he'd drive his cock into her with a vengeance. It was always the same, except for the stories she made up in her head or said aloud, and yet it never felt routinized or boring.

Dan sat on his knees, hunched forward, circled her clit with his fingers, then entered her, drawing out her juices and smearing them back over her clit. In and out, driving her to a frenzy. She watched his biceps flexing as his arm pumped up and down, like a miner digging for gold. His face held a look of intense concentration.

"What are you looking for?" she asked.

"Everything," he replied.

Everything she would give him. She thrust her hips forward, spread her legs as wide as they could possibly go, wanting to give him access to her deepest center. Sweat poured off his face and a lock of hair fell over his forehead. He threw his head back and kept pumping. Josie melted into the bed.

It didn't take long before she was out of her head. Finally: sweet relief. Nothing but flesh and fluids, no yesterday, no tomorrow, just here and now in her body. She could go on like this forever, never caring if she came, if he came, if the roof fell down on them.

But Dan always wanted her to come. And for that, Josie needed more than physical stimulation. She needed to pull her head back into the picture, to weave a psychological scenario. She wished that once, just once, she could come from physical sensation alone, spontaneously—but that was another of her sexual quirks she'd learned to accept, even enjoy.

"Take it, take everything out of me. I'm yours." She was whimpering now. "I'm where I'm supposed to be now. Just for you. Just for you."

Dan's cock was weeping tears of pre-come, but he would not enter her until he brought her to orgasm. He leaned forward to kiss her and she arched her head back, holding her neck up like an offering.

"Suck everything out of me," she groaned.

He sucked, hard, until she was begging him to bite her, to draw blood, to drink from her flesh. When he felt her pussy palpitating, he knew exactly what to do: holding his fingers motionless inside her, he pressed his thumb against her engorged clit, and she was coming, screaming indecipherable words, thrashing around, her cunt spasming. Only then did he climb up and put his cock into her, feeling her cunt clench him like a vise, and he pumped in and out, driving out her demons, driving himself so deep he almost vanished inside her, spilling his ejaculate into her accepting, willing cunt.

He collapsed on top of her. She stroked the back of his neck, his arms, his fingers, cooing the way she always did.

Josie's Rainy Day series of cards was growing at an unstoppable rate: her hands sketched clouds, storms at sea, hurricanes. The words she used to accompany the drawings now came only from herself, no quotes from Joni Mitchell or Bob Dylan, though it took great discipline to resist using "A Hard Rain's A-Gonna Fall." Nothing in the work suggested Dan, or sex, and yet it was, she knew, a direct outgrowth of their sex. A nagging fear lurked over her shoulder, that distributors wouldn't like the sad messages she was writing inside the cards, but she could not help herself. Perhaps they'd have to serve as sympathy cards for mourners of the dead. She consoled herself with the notion that the world needed some genuine expressions of grief.

She worked furiously, eight or ten hours at a stretch, breaking only to eat or to masturbate. She had learned early in life that when she was working, she had to take orgasm breaks: the creative impulse at its best flooded her with excitement that inevitably centered in her genitals. Thank god for the new flood of women's erotica—though she was not averse to the raunchiness of *Screw* or *Hustler*—and thank god for her Hitachi wand. She'd force herself to keep working beyond the initial surge of sexual excitement, to pour that energy into her art, but sooner or later she'd rush to the bed with a book and the vibrator. Coming in this way never interfered with her lust for Dan; they were entirely different experiences. So when he showed up a few hours later, she was happy to see him.

Dan had been thinking a lot about Josie's fertile sexual imagination, a new phenomenon he was fascinated by—but he also suspected that Josie's fantasies limited her. She'd hinted that she wished she could come "spontaneously," as a purely physical act, without a melodrama going on in her head. He'd decided to take this as a challenge: he would be the first man to drive Josie out of her mind. The prospect gave him a sense of power: compared to Josie, he was a sexual naif, and she had taught him much. Yet as experienced as she was—she'd been with dozens of men from all walks of life, plus a few women—she was so hung up in her head she could not come from physical sensation alone. With all she'd done for him, he wanted to do this for her, to give her something. Something that would make her remember him as special, that would make him stand out from all the rest. Not that he had a clear idea about how to accomplish this goal, but perhaps if he tried new and innovative positions he'd succeed where lesser men had failed.

She didn't send him away; in fact, she was in an upbeat mood and glad to see him. They shared half a bottle of wine before retiring to the bed. There, he went down on her for what felt like hours, persisting even when she pushed him away, saying it was too intense. Finally, out of sheer exhaustion, he lifted her so that her pelvis was sprawled across his legs, her breast near his mouth, and reached into the vast mysterious space of her cunt. In this position he found he could dig deeper than ever before. She was wet and wide open after his oral efforts, and she strained against him, gripping the back of his head to her breast, which he sucked and bit, eliciting deep grunts and groans.

Suddenly Josie's body went rigid. "Stop," she said, clawing at his arm. He didn't stop. "Please, stop, it's too much, I can't take it." Dan dove deeper, harder. Maybe he was hurting her; he didn't care. He'd reached some place where he'd never been, perhaps a place no one had ever been, and he wasn't about to leave it so easily.

"Dan, you have to *stop*!"

She twisted away from him, but he followed, his hand never leaving her cunt. She turned her back to him, reared up on her knees, and let out a howl of agony.

He felt something give way inside her, and then liquid was pouring all over his hand, down his arm, soaking the sheets. Jesus. What had he done? Ruptured her bladder? Terrified, he slowly withdrew his hand. Josie leaned forward as fluid continued to dribble down her thighs.

"I'll be damned," she whispered. "I guess it's true."

"What? What's true?" Dan's erection had shrunk like a deflated balloon. He stared at the spreading wetness on the sheets.

"I think I just ejaculated," she said proudly.

"Huh? Women don't ejaculate."

"Yeah, they do. Or so they say. I don't know, maybe I peed." She buried her nose in the sheets and sniffed. "Doesn't smell like pee."

Tentatively Dan leaned down and smelled it himself. It definitely did not smell like piss—more like seawater. He looked at Josie in amazement. Was she something other than human? A mermaid, perhaps? He could believe it of her.

"Wait," she said, and got out of bed, returning with a book containing those ridiculous diagrams they showed you in seventh grade. Hastily she turned to the chapter on "The G-Spot." He'd heard of the G-spot—but what did it have to do with this onrush of fluid?

Patiently she showed him the diagram, made him read the text on female ejaculation.

"I didn't believe it either—but there it is," she said, pointing to the wet sheets. She collapsed then. "God, that was exhausting."

Dan put the book aside and looked at Josie: her face was a study in blissful contentment, the lines around her mouth and eyes relaxed. But for her gray hair, she looked like a teenager.

"Come over here," she said, putting an arm around him. He snuggled next to her breast and she held on to him, stroking his hair and cooing. "The amazing thing," she said, her voice filled with awe, "is that it was totally spontaneous. I didn't need a story. I wasn't thinking any words. I wasn't thinking at all." Emotions emanated from her pores like waves washing over him. Gratitude. Love. Wonder. Relief.

"You haven't come," she said softly.

"It's okay. I don't have to."

"You sure?"

"Maybe later."

He held her as she drifted into peaceful sleep. He wiggled his fingers, feeling the power in his hands—the power to drive from this complicated woman all thought and language, to bring her to a purely physical state of literal meltdown.

She stirred. "What are you thinking?" she murmured, half asleep.

"I kind of like being a Rainy Day Man."

Addiction

WILLIAM R. BURKETT, JR.

WARM JUNE EVENING ON THE BOULEVARD; EVERY CAFÉ HAS ITS street side opened up to the sidewalk, and the outside tables are full. The pedestrian throng passes in and out of the orange glow of corner street lamps, moving shadows against the multi-colored neon of shop windows. Mating rituals are in full swing: hetero, male on male, female on female; ménage à trois. Couples gaze into each other's eyes across tiny tables, others prank and prance down the pavements. In attire, they run the gamut from haute couture to extras in the street scenes from *Blade Runner*.

I sit with my back to a sturdy brick column in front of the coffee shop. My privacy bubble is a translucent shroud around the tabletop and my hands on this keyboard. Only my eyeglasses have the code-chip to cut the shimmer and let me see this screen. Nor can any lurking hacker bounce a signal through the bubble to pirate images from my screen. Computer security has come a long way.

I could be working on proprietary business data, or composing limpid prose. But I'm not. I'm on-line, though since the digital and bandwidth breakthroughs late in the twentieth century, "line" is an anachronistic term.

My heart is sore; that is the only way I know to describe it. Physically and emotionally sore. The nitro capsules lie beside this keyboard, just in case. I hate those things: instant migraine! And I have battled migraines far longer in my life than a stumbling heart.

—*You are quiet tonight.*

The words appear on my screen in a "window" identified by a screen name. My heart jumps. My sweet D has found me once again. The magic of the computer age: intimate contact across a continent, or ocean. Swift rapport, almost telepathic in its intensity. No risk of disease, no messy exchange of body fluids, no risk at all. Except heartbreak.

My fingers flicker. —*Yes. Quiet.*

—*Tired? Sad? Heartsick?*

—*Some of each*, I type.

—*Then let me take you to our special place and heal you.*

My fingers hesitate. Then:—*I'm not sure I can be healed.*

—*Come, my precious love . . .*

In my privacy sphere, the screen changes. As through an actual window, I look into the fantasy flat that she and I have decorated across the months. The Empire writing desk she purchased for me on Quai d'Orsay. The floral-patterned wicker couch where first we consummated our virtual love. Beyond the couch, the glass doors give onto the balcony. I can see the reflected glow of Paris, and remember the time I took her from the rear, her breasts scraping the cold brick as she bit her lip to keep from crying out. In real life, Paris is over six thousand miles from my sidewalk chair, and she lives somewhere in the urban sprawl along the old Post Road between Boston and Manhattan.

D: *There's huge thunderstorms going on here . . . you know that makes me happy.*

Me: *Threat to your machine?*

D: *Who cares? It's fabulous!*

Me: *My stormy darling.*

D: *Are you all right, sweet? You seem . . . not yourself.*

Me: *Kind of tired . . .*

D: *All right . . . you walk in the door . . . exhausted after a long day . . . I can see the weariness in your eyes . . .*

Me: *Truly.*

D: *Take off your jacket and follow me into the bath. . . . I have a surprise. Only now do you realize the scent wafting through our apartment is fresh-cut flowers . . .*

Me: *<tiredly> Mmmm.*

D: *I bought some at a stand near the entrance to the Metro today. They were so bright and beautiful that I HAD to have them. I have candles lit around the bath also, freesia-scented. Very invigorating yet soothing. A scent which awakens you . . .*

Me: *Oh D, this is what I need.*

I have woven so many virtual dreams across the years for on-line lovers. They called me their dreamweaver. But only D seems able to sense when my yarn is spent, and then she takes up the thread.

—*Let me take your clothes off . . . your shirt . . . hold you close a moment . . . kiss you. Then I undo your trousers, and you step out of them, shoes and socks kicked off now. Step inside the tub . . . the water is warm and soothing. The perfect temperature. Lay back and close your eyes while I bathe you . . . just breathe . . . dream. Feel good?*

And it does. I am sitting in jeans and a polo shirt, watching the passing pedestrians in a soft warm night. D is a continent away, her apartment windows rattling in a thunderstorm. But despite my melancholy I am transported to our Paris flat by the old sweet magic. I can feel her hands on me, see her glowing eyes. I feel the old hot stirring in my loins.

D: *I have a soft washcloth . . . start at your neck, gently scrubbing, cleansing . . . the water feels so good. I have a robe . . . silk . . . very loose at the bodice. It hides nothing. I lean over to get closer to you. . . . You reach for my breasts, very visible. Mmmmm . . . so exciting. My nipples harden immediately.*

In my mind's eye, I see them, nudging up stiff and proud. There was a time when my pulse would have raced madly in response to this scene my faraway lover builds for me. She is financially well-off, happily married, far younger than I, and bursting with barely restrained eroticism. I am an aging writer, stone-broke again. My mind is the only organ left in my body that quivers to erotic overtures. If you don't count my stumbling heart.

D and I have never seen each other. Never touched. Never will. We have agreed to forgo the modern software that would permit us to see each other in living motion, full sound and color, right down to erections and sexual flushes of the flesh. We don't even actually achieve orgasm, as many do in here. Well, I don't, and she says she never does. We share a simple love of language and the evocative magic of words. In another age, we might have been pen pals, waiting impatiently for the mail ship or the Pony Express rider. Some exquisite erotic correspondences survive from the era of the quill pen and hot wax seal. Our lives connect only here, tenuously, and yet with a strange power. It truly is modern magic.

And this magic has its price.

I open a separate search window—a slightly illegal program for a civilian to have—and find her on-line. That is, I find which other features of the on-line software she is engaged in at this moment. This once was top-secret police software, now downloadable from offshore for a fee. Official regulators have pretty much given up attempts to monitor this medium.

D is connected to one of her private domination fantasy rooms. Perhaps wielding a virtual whip across the buttocks of one of her other lovers, chained to a dungeon wall. Or romping in a virtual ménage, wildly orgasmic, her imagination stuffed with male flesh. My fingers hover, ready to key the "back door" that will let me look inside her fantasy unobserved. Instead, I free my hands from the sphere and sip my coffee, feeling the old pain rise again.

She says she loves me.

And I have vowed the same to her. Once, while I simultaneously seduced an on-line virgin in an adjacent window. I doubted by then there was such a thing as an on-line virgin, and even wondered if my new conquest was truly female. But the idea of seduction—while vowing love to D—was so powerfully erotic I could not resist. The answer to both my questions about the virgin proved to be yes, eventually. My heart grew even heavier when this latest conquest— the decorous wife of a Mormon elder—began to write me erotic love poems. D found it exciting when I finally told her.

D: *I stand up . . . undo the sash on the robe . . . it drops to the floor, around my feet. I step out of it.*

She and I used to make jokes about simultaneous cyberplay. Multitasking, we called it, in the cynical jargon of cyberia. In an unguarded moment, she confided she could keep four separate erotic scenes in play at once. Which made her so horny and aroused that her poor husband never had a chance when he got home from the stock exchange. Lately she has been teasing him about their mutual friend across the hall, a voluptuous blonde. She is considering involving him in a real life ménage à trois. His reward, she says coyly, for being her virtual cuckold.

She tells me these things, expecting my approval. Yet she says she loves me. And how can I deny her? My tattered old heart leaped when she found me. I long since have stopped multitasking when I am with her. A secret act of fealty. I yearn to tell her, and ask for her reciprocation—but fear she will vanish off my screen forever if I do. Her lifemate's possessiveness of her is the only thing about him she despises. In bitter irony, I feel a kind of brotherhood with him. She still is in her private orgy. But at the same time:

D: *I place one foot in the tub, by your right hip. Now the other, by your left. I slowly lower myself into the tub . . . into the water. ONTO you. Your hands are on my hips. I lean forward, my breasts against your chest. My head on your shoulder . . .*

And I can feel her there. Feel the soft roundness of her hips, the brush of her done-up hair against my cheek, her lips nuzzling me. I shiver, though the June night is warm. My chest tingles as if I can feel her nipples there, branding me.

Me: *Your nipples are so hard, my love.*

D: *Mmmm, yes . . . because of you. So nice here. Just relax, my love . . . the day is gone and we're together now. This is all the world we need now. I feel your hardness. Can we be any closer?*

Me: *Only if . . .*

D: *Tell me.*

Me: *Put your hands on me and guide me into you. Your warm soapy hands.*

D: *Squeezing my slippery hands down your hot wet shaft. Centering you, rubbing you back and forth as I lower myself, soooo slow. Feel my warmth engulf you. Oh! You are so very hard now. Hard and deep. My love, let down my hair . . .*

She knows I love that image, of her long hair coming loose, cascading over me, secluding her face in erotic shadow.

Me: *Fingers trembling. But I manage . . .*

My fingers are trembling, in fact. I have to erase a typo twice.

D: *I shake my head to let it all drop, all around your face. You manage well at many things, darling. Kiss me hard. Hard on the mouth.*

Me: *While you impale yourself on me . . .*

I can feel her now—truly feel her—so that my hips roll on the coffee-shop chair as if thrusting up. I can feel my testicles draw up, tight, and a shadow of the old hard ache of real-life lust floods me.

D: *I feel you thrusting up. Oh yes! Mmmm. My head goes back and your mouth finds my breasts.*

I am no longer surprised when she anticipates my words. Reality flickers and fades, and we are there, together, in the warm soapy water, bodies moving as one. My lips move almost unconsciously, shaping around a nipple three thousand miles away.

Me: *Sucking you gently into my mouth . . . mmm . . . a random taste of soap . . . and I nibble, scraping your erect flesh with my teeth.*

D: *Oooh. <gasping> YES. Biting my lip for some semblance of control. Oh god, my love . . .*

Me: *Teeth sinking into your rigid flesh. Hands kneading you. My hips thrusting up to you.*

D: *Deeper! Yes! Oh—OH! So good, love, so good. Tell me what you want . . . what you need from me.*

Me: *I want you to come—hard—over and over . . .*

D: *I am yours. Oh god. Oh—god! My breasts heaving for air; holding you. YES! YES, YES.*

Me: *Driving up. Deep . . . throbbing . . . reaching your very bottom.*

D: *Yesssss. . . . As I ride you so hard! The water splashes everywhere. We don't care! Candles sizzle from the splashes. Oh, my lover—DO me! Fuck me! Oh god . . . Holding you so close. Oh god! I'm going to—*

We are into it now, and I don't care where I am or where she is in actual fact. All that exists is this sloshing tub, the heavy, hot, almost tidal shift of the tub water over our joined bodies.

Me: *I feel you, love. Yes, love. Yes. Now!*

D: *I'm going to come. God! Yes! Yes!*

Me: *Holding there—holding DEEP. Swelling . . .*

D: *Oh god! I'm whimpering. Again . . . again. I can't stop. Oh I can't. I can't! Again!!! Oh, CHRIST! Come for me . . . come in me!*

Me: *Are you sure, love? I can hold . . .*

And once upon a time, I could. Vivid memories meld with fantasy, and it feels like my body is levitating out of the chair. My entire essence, whatever is the *me* in this aging body, seems to flow away from me, away—perhaps into electrons, flashing across the miles.

Me: *Now! Now, Baby! Hard and hot and splashing . . . it's now!*

D: *Let me feel you! I'm going crazy! You're making me CRAZY.*

Me: *Exploding. BURSTING . . . filling you.*

D: *Oh god! I can feel you . . . inside me . . . I feel you letting go! So real, so real. My god! I feeeeel you! And oh! AGAIN!*

The cursor flickers quietly for a long moment, time for my heart to beat a dozen times at this accelerated pace. I am breathing unevenly through my mouth. Finally:

D: *Breathing slower . . . easier now . . .*

Me: *Come down here and let me hold you.*

D: *My heart is pounding so hard. I can feel yours too! Mmmm, yes—hold me. Ohhhhhh . . . the best arms. The safest and warmest love . . .*

Me: *Safe and warm, love. Sighhhh. In this strange universe, all things are possible. Even that you love an old guy like me . . .*

D: *Old guys like you, but especially you, turn me on big-time.*

Me: *Moving to the top of your dance card?*

D: *You are at the top! Go and get some sleep, love, and dream of me a little . . .*

And she is gone from my screen, back to her other private fantasy. D never has bothered to create a separate screen name for her dalliances . . .

I become aware of the street scene again. A lithe woman, with gray at her blond temples, and jaded eyes, catches my glance. She quirks a somehow sardonic eyebrow. Every passerby must have known what I was doing. My face is hot and flushed, and I can feel sweat on my forehead. There's a damp spot on my jeans. The nose-pierced male waiter replenishes my coffee; even he gives me the once-over. I must be leaking pheromones into the night air. A false signal. There is moisture, but no lingering tumescence, in my nether regions.

Behind my ribs, my heart gives a keen squeeze. The glowing screen seems to darken. The passing parade fades into a flicker of phantoms. I breathe cautiously, needing air, but afraid to suck it deep. Afraid a deep inhale will trigger—something final. I hold the pill bottle in my hand. I'd almost rather die than trigger another migraine.

I check my search program again. D is still happily ensconced. My fevered imagination conjures strings of depraved words. My sweet D, debased and debasing. Green jealousy flashes through me like fire—all the hotter because I am as guilty as she. Perhaps guiltier.

My melancholy settles more closely around me. How on earth did I come to this?

My first real-time lover was gentle and erotic, and awakened me to the full magic of the flesh. It was an intoxicating discovery that I immediately yearned to share with every woman I met. I eventually married and stayed faithful to my one and only wife for seven good years. A pathetic Hollywood joke, that seven-year itch, but it gouged unsealable cracks in our relationship, and I was alone again, with no idea how to approach women anymore, and little desire to try.

Then came the on-line services, outrageously expensive in the early days, difficult to keep a connection—and addictive. I didn't stop at one on-line affair, or two, or ten. More than one of my lovers—for I somehow always seemed to find bright, intuitive women—believed I was just in love with love. But my heart could not, and cannot, seem to tell the difference.

I proceeded to telephone sex, then to a real-time rendezvous. Fell in love with this woman that my typing had summoned into real-life as magically as some sorcerer's spell. She wanted me to turn off the computer, turn my back on my on-line affairs. Before I could manage to do that, she left me, her heart torn to pieces. I mourned her loss—and returned to the Net. Became a dreamweaver for so many lonely ladies.

A cooling wind sweeps down the Boulevard. My heart speaks to me again beneath my ribs. Not in the romantic language of love, but the flesh reality of impending mortality. The medics say I really have nothing to worry about: sound genetic stock, a solid exercise program, proper diet. I should last a long time. But my heart and I know better. It is sore from too much giving, too much taking.

My screen chimes. Words appear, as if by magic.

—*I was hoping you would be here. I can't think of anything but you. Just seeing your screen name on-line makes me go all wet and yearning.*

My old heart lurches painfully. —*Hello, my darling A. How's your weather there?*

—*Cold and snowing. It's winter down in the southern hemisphere, you know. I am sitting by the fireplace. In our special cabin in the mountains. The fire is so cozy, all I have on is this old T-shirt you snail-mailed me last year. You know how easily that comes off . . .*

The pedestrians parade by. The hour is growing late. My coffee is cold. I close my eyes and see A there, a world away, where the water runs anti-clockwise down the drains. Her breasts fill my old Mariners shirt, her eyes glow in the firelight. When I open my eyes, new words have appeared on the screen.

—*You seem quiet tonight, my precious dreamweaver. Are you okay?*

I squeeze my eyes shut again. I can't do this anymore. But my fingers move in their practiced rituals, almost independent of me.

—*Just lonesome. For you.*

—*Then come into my arms, and I will warm you.*

My fickle heart suddenly is quiet, as if listening. I signal for more coffee, and begin to type.

Fisherman's Friend

TABITHA FLYTE

THE FISHERMAN JERKED HIS ROD. AT LAST HE HAD CAUGHT something. He hooked the fish and pulled it in triumphantly. Even from ten yards away I could hear how the line strained. The poor creature didn't have a chance. The fisherman's biceps bulged as he worked the reel. He had a lithe body, sloping shoulders, sleek and damp like a water sprite. Tears of water, little beads of sweat, clung to his toned chest. His skin was so smooth, almost inviting touch. His hair glittered black-purple in the shafts of sunlight, and his toes made sweet indentations in the sand. I wanted to touch him.

The fish swung toward the fisherman, and he caught it. Carefully, he unhooked it, and then euphorically, he squeezed his prey. It flopped and jittered in his hard-working hands.

I clapped approvingly so that he would know that I was impressed. As usual, he only nodded solemnly back at me. He dunked the fish in the plastic bucket, and I walked away, red-faced and lonely.

"I want to learn how to fish," I announced the next day. The fisherman hadn't taken off his shirt, but he still looked delectable.

"You?" he asked with a rare grin. "What do you know about fish?"

"Nothing, but I'm willing to learn."

He shrugged. "Do you want to be good at it, or just mediocre?"

"Good, of course!"

"Then you're not ready."

"Why not?"

"You don't have the most important quality."

"What's the most important quality?"

"Patience," he said. His eyes were twinkling. I had the feeling that he was mocking me. He started unbuttoning his shirt. Each button seemed to tremble under his fingers. I stayed by him. When he looked up, he seemed surprised that I was still there.

I sat nearby so that I could watch his movements. He never looked pleased or displeased to see me; he didn't pay me any attention at all. He would roll up his trousers, revealing suntanned legs covered with fine downy hair. Then he would pad across the sand to immerse his feet in the sea. Sometimes he picked up stones, weighing them in his hands, as if deciding their power, and then he would swing his arms and release the stones across the harbor. They made splashing sounds. One time he stripped down to a tiny pair of trunks and ran, bullet-fast, into the waves. He disappeared for so long that I held my breath, fearing that he was dead, but then he reemerged a few yards away, his hair shiny and his face triumphant. He swam strong, heavy strokes and I marveled at the strength of his torso, his powerful kicks, and his obvious ease in the water.

Usually, though, he just stood still at the water's edge, holding the fishing rod and waiting. He looked like he was playing musical statues, when the music stops and you freeze.

Maybe he was praying for a bite. I don't know.

I tried to look as attractive and as interested as I could. But I grew restless.

One afternoon I asked if I could help. He pretended reluctance, so I grabbed the rod from him.

"Whoa, easy," he said, "you can't treat it like that."

"How, then?" I pouted.

He looped his arms around me from behind and steadied the equipment. I felt how warm and wide his chest was, and I stopped struggling.

I hadn't been that close to a man in a long time.

I tried to lean back into him, but he wasn't having any of it. He said that I had a lot to learn. His arms were huge. I felt a kind of hunger in my chest.

"Patience," he reminded me, "plus there are other things too."

When he was reeling in, I realized that I had clumsily tangled his line.

"Such as?"

"You have to be good with your hands. . . ."

I watched his agile hands. How would they feel, rubbing the inside of my legs, creeping up my thighs?

"And sensitive, and resourceful."

"I am all that and more," I boasted.

He was laughing at me. His eyelashes stuck together in glistening dark clumps.

"We'll see," he said.

I swam directly opposite him. He wanted to cast out a line, but I was in his way. He shrugged his shoulders at the obstruction and simply prepared some more bait. I was fed up with being ignored. I felt the water slip-slide around my body, giving me courage, so I came out of the sea up to the edge where the water just about caressed my toes. Trembling, I stood up. The sun was behind him and I had to squint to see.

I shook my hair and slowly, very slowly, drew my right swimsuit strap down. I pushed it down my upper arm, and then I did the same on my left side. First my right breast and then my left was exposed. The sun caressed my naked flesh. Pretty tears of water clung to my tits. He was ahead of me, blurry and unfocused. "Look at me," I whispered, "please see me and want me."

The curvy clouds moved fast across the bold blue sky. The swimsuit was down my middle, revealing little inside-out flowers. I slid the swimsuit over the chunk of my hips, down to the first sightings of my pubic hair. I paused, feeling the dampness of the cloth stir my excitement. Down, down, down it went to my thighs, to rest indecorously on my knees, and then I stepped out of it, leaving the material on the sand. I became aware of the tiniest sensations, the feel of my shoulders, my tongue between my front teeth, even the air from my nose. My hair was wet on my back, causing drops of water to land plump on my shivering buttocks. I could feel warm arousal flooding my sex.

When I looked up, he was still threading the worm through his hook.

He said that they were going out on a boat. I could go with them if I wanted. He thought I was getting the hang of things. He had crooked teeth and a lopsided smile and there was something about his eyes that made him look like he was about to cry.

It was a small boat, and it was soon filled with bulky equipment and buckets of small fish to catch bigger fish with. He was superstitious. He said that he was wearing red shorts for good luck. I hoped that he would fish well enough to want to take me with him again.

The smooth motion of the water calmed me, and I was happy. My fisherman was even more handsome when he concentrated. A furrow, a single worry line creased his forehead. Sometimes he looked over at me and smiled.

One of the fishermen caught a pike. The other men crowded around him, thumping his shoulders. Then the fish leaped up in the air, a last gasp, but my fisherman caught it deftly. He kissed its slimy surface.

I would have done anything to have been that fish, to be caught, to be gutted and served up for his tea.

The fisherman sat next to me and asked if I was enjoying myself. He smelled of the sea, and white salt had stuck to his neck from the wind's blowing water at him.

"I'm trying to be patient." I sounded shrill and girlish. He touched the small of my back. A light pressure, two fingers and a thumb.

We still haven't kissed each other yet, I thought. But I felt like I was melting.

"You looked beautiful in your swimming costume."

"I didn't think you noticed."

"I noticed. . . . You looked even better with nothing on."

"I'm wearing a bikini underneath today," I said coyly.

"Why don't you take it off?" he said.

I looked up at him to see if he was joking, but his face was serious. I could feel his breath on my ear.

"What about them?"

I gestured to the men talking fish and walking around in squelchy sandals.

"They won't see."

I unlaced the bikini top and pulled it through the sleeve of my T-shirt. I was wearing a skirt, so removing the bikini bottoms was easier. Locking his eyes, I wriggled out of the briefs and stuffed them hurriedly in my bag.

"There!" I chirped. My face was flushed, and I felt giddy. He rested his hand on my knee, nonchalantly, as if it could have been anyone's. I liked the way his fingers looked there.

I had to take slow deep breaths. I watched the slip tide. The waves grew larger and more passionate, as though they were competing spirits.

He was concerned because I was trembling so much. "Seasick?"

"No," I protested. "Just . . . excited."

The motion of the boat felt nice on my bottom. If I opened my legs just slightly I could feel air rush up my sex. It reminded me of a time, a prehistoric time, when I had made love against a washing machine. Its cold vibrating surface had rubbed and stoked a violently passionate response.

I wondered if he could read my mind; he looked as though he might. Our thighs rubbed together.

"Sometimes even the most patient fisherman has to accept that he can't make a catch," he said.

"Not me; I'm persevering."

He kissed me for the first time. He kissed me full on the lips. Then our lips parted gently and we were openmouthed, needy. His tongue was warm and wet in my mouth. I felt hot and pushed myself against him. The boat lurched and covered us in cool spray like spittle. We laughed so loudly that the other fishermen turned around and asked us what was so funny.

We landed at a bay for a break. The boat seemed to tug away but the anchor clung on and the boat was soon tamed. All the fishermen made off for one side of the rocks, but he held back and took me to the other.

"Still excited?" he whispered.

I nodded slowly. I didn't trust myself to speak. He was still wearing his tight T-shirt, and his nipples grazed its flimsy cotton. We sat close together on the sand and I was embarrassed at the knickers-less proximity. No, thank you, he didn't want any suntan lotion. No, he didn't want any coffee. I poured myself a drink from my flask. The thick liquid sloshed and gurgled in the cup. I rubbed lotion on my legs, feeling the sliding oil seep into my skin.

He lay back with his arms behind his head, and I knew that he was watching me.

I stared ahead into the endless sea rather than look at him.

"Touch yourself," he said abruptly.

"What?"

"I want you to play with yourself."

There were other people around. Just seconds away there were fishermen eating lunch.

"Not here."

"They won't see," he said. "You have to learn how to be good with your hands."

I slid my hands down my skirt and felt my welcoming pubic mound. I looked up at him for approval, and he nodded, licking his lips. I felt my slit moisten and contract. It was actually a relief to finally insert my finger, but I wasn't going to admit it.

"Open your legs. I can't see properly."

I parted my thighs just slightly, but he rolled down and over so that he was eye to eye with my pussy. I felt awkward and naked, like a Christmas tree without lights.

"Wider," he insisted. I obeyed fearfully. My cunt was drenching my finger. I added a second digit for good measure, but I was still ashamed.

"Please touch me," I requested weakly. I couldn't bear his window-shopping.

"Patience," he whispered.

I masturbated. I was reluctant at first, but then I couldn't stop. It was fantastic to have an audience, and his face, so keenly admiring, made me more confident. My hole was soaking eagerness. I wanted to show him more, to turn him on as much as I could. I squeezed my breasts, offering him the sight of my red nipples. I devoted most of my attention to the cove between my legs, wetter than the ocean, sweeter than a kiss. My thumb found my clitoris and I whisked my fingers up and down.

He was hard. His trousers tented forward at the groin.

I was getting faster, rattling my fingers up my creaminess. I was whispering, "Yes, please, yes."

He put his finger over my lips. They were nearby, *shhhhh*, but I suckled his finger and continued to moan. Part of me, I suppose, could have quieted down, but the other part was urging more drama.

Suddenly he lunged forward, pushing his face to my pussy. He was under me, buried under my skirt, lapping at me as firm and fast as the waves lapping at the shore. He opened my legs even wider, so that I was split, spread beaver. Oh god, anyone could have seen or heard if they wanted to, but I couldn't stop. I had the catch of the year. I clapped my legs over his shoulders and held the back of his head tight. His tongue was jammed up me and I wouldn't let him go. I thrust my buttocks at him, and he slipped one hand under each cheek, rubbing his face euphorically in my soaking hollow.

"Oh yes, oh yes," I bellowed. I was going to be the best fucking fisherwoman in the world. I sprang up and down on his face, howling for more. *Don't stop, don't ever stop, yes, YES!* My body and my brain were located in that small hot place between my legs. I didn't care who was watching, all I cared was that he stayed attached to me, kept giving me these unbelievable pleasures.

When eventually he emerged, his cheeks, his nose, his chin were glistening with my come.

On the boat ride back he said I should get used to the water. I knelt up on the bench, leaned over the side, and let the wetness glide over my fingers. He stood behind me, massaging my shoulders. When I pressed against him I could feel the rigidity of his shaft.

The other fishermen were talking about the size of their fish. It had been a good day. My fisherman agreed. The fish were biting, he said. Their voices washed over me. My fisherman moved his hands under my sweater and cupped my breasts. He twiddled my nipples. He snaked a way under my skirt. He was still talking with them about the trip as he slid his fingers over my buttocks. He murmured that I mustn't move. Don't be afraid. His hand explored my underside, heading for where his mouth had been earlier, and I groaned quietly, my sighs lost in the wind, pushing back on him encouragingly. The waves pressed at the side of the boat while he surged up and down me, up and down my hole.

When he removed his finger, disappointment rippled through me, but I knew that he was right. We had to stop. I didn't want to get into trouble.

"Wait," he whispered though. He rifled through my bag and took out the suntan lotion. For a second I thought he was going to oil me, god knows why, I was as wet as they come, but then the bottle disappeared up my skirt. Deftly, he opened my legs wider, and I felt a sudden shock as he slid the tube up me.

"Catch anything, Marty?" he yelled to a mate. I knew he was just showing off, playing a silly game, but I loved it. I had to be silent, but I wanted to scream my orgasm to the world. He worked the lotion bottle up and down. It was just a little too big, but that was the way I liked it. I was bobbing around like a buoy. I was scared they would hear, I was right next to them, pretending to be sane, but I couldn't stop, *more, please, more.* I was coming again.

Oh god.

Afterward he showed me how his fingers were crinkled like raisins.

The following day the sky was dark and overcast. He said there would be no boat trip, we would have to fish off the coast. Before I could touch his equipment, he said, there was more to learn.

"But . . ." I began impetuously, then saw he was laughing at me. "What will you teach me today?"

"Courage and trust," he said.

I couldn't help grinning.

First we swam. I wrapped my legs around him in the ocean. I could feel his hardness in the soft water and I clung weightless to his firm body. I tried to force his pants down, but he clutched them to him, prudish. For me, though, the rules were different. He unfastened my bikini top, and dove underwater to suck my nipples. They were as hard as little shells. He made me take off my bikini bottoms. My thighs gleamed luminous white. It was strange to touch my cunt in the water, to feel the wetness there, different from the wetness around me.

When we left the sea, I had goose pimples. He wrapped me in a big fluffy towel and I felt cared for and loved like a baby.

"Go and lie down," he said.

"I don't want to, the fishermen are just over there."

He stared at me closely. My cunt stirred. I didn't want to get caught, but I liked that we might.

We kissed longingly, lingeringly. He swirled patterns of eight in my mouth. I was aggressive, forcing his tongue inside me and insisting our mouths widen. My upper lips mirrored what I wanted lower down. He slid his tongue over my breasts and nibbled at my nipples. I cram-fed my tits into his mouth. I rubbed his face in them. I think he liked it, I hardly cared whether he did or not.

"Open your legs," he said, and once again, I parted my thighs willingly. *See how red and wet my slit is!* I lay back, ready to be serviced. *I could get used to this,* I thought.

"Wait there," he said, and he was up and running again.

He came back with fishing line and hooks. He put me in a starfish shape, my legs and arms akimbo, and then he tied me up. He promised it wouldn't be for long, but I didn't mind. Within the restrictions, I was free to come as hard as I liked.

"You look so horny," he said.

I felt so horny. My exposed pussy was soaking.

I started to move my pelvis. I can only imagine how hot it must have looked; my legs bent to accommodate him, my sex open wide and ready for action. I started to pump, to grind. I was split open for him, all for him. I gyrated, aware only of the space that needed filling. *Feed me, please, and I will tighten and fuck you like you've never been fucked before.*

I tried to hump the air. I needed something up there.

"Please," I groaned, anything would do.

I felt his finger make its persuasion up me, and I rubbed against it happily. His thumb wandered up the slick of my vagina and landed warmly on my clitoris.

I raised my bottom, up and down, giving it to him. Putting on a show for him.

"Oh baby, you're so fucking hot."

"Fuck me now."

Then I heard voices. If I could have, I would have whipped on my clothes, covered up my pubic hair and my breasts. I would have run away, fleeing into the sea. Perhaps I would have drowned in shame. As it was, I couldn't move, I was stuck revealing all my goods.

There were two of his mates, wandering around, admiring his catch.

"Don't worry about them."

He snaked his long tongue in my mouth, but I whipped my head from side to side.

"No, no."

"It's all right, just relax."

I couldn't. Not yet, not now, but his hands were on my thighs, massaging the tender spot between leg and hole, and I felt my resistance waning. All I wanted was some reassurance, and he gave me that readily.

I let his finger wander inside me. I rocked with his invading hand, feeling the tide of my enjoyment. I was getting off on his frigging finger. I was proud of it too, proud that I was so hot, so ready. I liked the way I looked; all genitalia exposed. I was better than their wives and girlfriends, hotter than anyone they'd seen before.

"Oh yes, you dirty woman," he encouraged. He wanted me to come in front of his friends. "Legs wider. Show them your cunt. Show them how much you love it."

I wanted them to see how horny I was. I strained to let them see my wetness.

"You little slut," he said admiringly.

One hand was tiptoeing on my nipples. The other was vibrating my clitoris, making me breathless.

"You want them, don't you?"

He knew I wanted it more than anything and there was no way I could say no. Three men touching me, three gorgeous men fondling little old me. What had I done to deserve this? But I couldn't say yes. I showed my assent in other ways. I moved my pussy frantically against his hand. I finger-fucked faster. I loved the anticipation on my audience's faces.

Then someone else's sandy hands were on my tits, massaging me tight. Someone else had sneaked his hands around to fondle my ass. I closed my eyes and wriggled like a newly caught fish, only I had never felt more alive. Each man had a finger in my honey pot. My mouth was bubbling uncontrollably. My fisherman put his finger between my lips, and I sucked him vigorously, grazing him with my teeth. I didn't know what was what and who was who anymore.

One of the men maneuvered himself on top of me. He raised my pelvis to equal his. I was scared that he wouldn't last long because he was almost moaning his orgasm even as his cock's tip touched my entrance. Then, as I felt the cock soar up me, I had to close my eyes. His prick was so big. It bashed against my pussy walls, going deeper than I expected. I could almost feel it ramming between my kidneys.

Let them see what I was made of.

The other stranger sucked my nipples. He treated them with such attention, such showering love, that I clutched him to them, sighing that he must do it forever. Then he, too, was on top of me, thrusting his cock at my breasts, tit-fuck.

My beautiful fisherman watched me approvingly as I grimaced and thrusted. Then he undid his shorts. There was only one place for him to go. He held his cock out beseechingly, and I gobbled it up, gagging on it happily.

I was not going to come first. Not me, not me—but as each shove splintered my clit and filled my void, my resistance was battered down. I pushed harder against the cock inside my sex. The stranger responded, picking up my buttocks and hammering home. As the pleasures mounted, I could no longer work on the prick in my mouth, but let my lips lie slack as he surged in and out of my hole. His cock muffled my cries, but then my clit was off like a trigger, pulsating and rushing, and I set them all off. There was a series of exquisite thrusting and glorious explosions. My mouth, my breasts, and my slit were all filled with milky love juices.

"You still haven't fucked me properly yet," I scolded my fisherman the next day. "Or taught me how to fish."

"I still don't know if you are daring enough," he said.

After all I had done, he was questioning my courage!

He made me get on hands and knees in the warm water. Small stones dug into the palms of my hands. I allowed him to part my legs gently. He slapped my buttock cheeks until they stung. He was powerful. He would hunt and trap without asking.

"Look at your gorgeous ass."

I wriggled my backside delightedly.

He kissed me there, and I could feel my cunt swell with water. Water, water everywhere, and plenty a drop to drink. I wondered if he would lick me again. I had never been licked like that before, but his penis was banging against me, and we still hadn't fucked. I was dreaming of the final penetration, he and I would be hooked forever.

He molded my ass like he did that day on the boat, caressing the flesh, squeezing the base. I expected him to feel his way through to my cunt, but he didn't. Instead, he pulled at my buttocks, opening me wide, revealing my tiny hole to the world.

"What are you doing?"

He was silent. There was just the sound of the waves, amplified, as though I had put a shell to my ears.

"Hey!" Before I could protest, his finger was burrowing at my asshole. I shivered as it journeyed up me.

"Stop it," I hissed. I didn't want dirty and earthy.

The finger continued unhindered up my virgin backside.

"No," I whined.

Yet the invasion felt so delicious. The surf skimmed my nipples. As I breathed in and out, my breasts submerged and then emerged from the water. I tried to concentrate on them and not the pain. He was going where he shouldn't go. He stroked my hair. I sniffed in sea air.

I grew used to it. Very slowly and awkwardly, I moved against his finger, *oh yes.* The sea ebbed and flowed around me as I ebbed and flowed around him.

"You love it, baby," he said. I wanted to say no, but I would have been lying. The waves were washing against the rocks, smashing the rocks, chopping and changing their color and shape. There were fishermen on the shore just yards from us. What did I look like impaled on his finger, the sea behind me, his finger up me? I heard trousers unzipping. I heard an erect cock being pulled roughly from lucky red pants.

Oh god.

I knew what he was going to try and do even before he said it.

"I'm going to fuck you up the ass."

"No," I whimpered. I was just being practical. It wouldn't go up there.

"Oh baby, don't you trust me?" he asked. Large raindrops were pattering across my back and on the sea. It felt fantastic. Even the sky was abandoning itself, a benevolent release. But I was still afraid of nature.

"It's raining," I said feebly.

"Shhhushhhh, don't fight it." He searched and then knew how wet my clit was becoming.

"Oh yes, you *do* want me!"

"I don't," I said through gritted teeth.

I felt his erect cock press against my tiny puckered hole, and then it pressed farther, harder and deeper still, until it was fully submerged.

I could hear the fishermen clapping and whistling.

"Say it. You do want me!" he insisted.

I couldn't speak. I couldn't move. I waited, still as a fisherman. And he was massaging my cunt with one eager hand, and one hand was caressing a breast. He was moaning love words into my neck, I was gorgeous, the best, there was no one else and never would be. I waited until forever and the sea swirled around my legs, my arms, my tits, and I knew I would never be the same again.

"Say it," he begged.

"Yes." My voice was low and animal. It seemed to come from a different source. "*Yes*, fuck me *now*."

We were digging at each other, screwing madly. I was sawing at him, clamoring for more, insisting that he fuck me harder. My face grew flame-colored and my body liquid. We were no longer two separate solids, but we were fluid, sliding into each other, pouring into each other, becoming one unstoppable wave of pleasure. When he convulsed inside my too-tight passage, I jerked and flailed, but I wanted us to go on forever. I felt wetness all around and didn't know if it was my sticky juice, or his, or if it was nothing to do with us. I howled like a sea monster, screaming explicitly and storming as he exploded up me again and violently again.

Then he wiped the sweat off his beautiful brow, and we walked back to the shoreline to the applause of the others. The fisherman closed me tight in his arms and squeezed me euphorically. I just flopped and jittered in his hard-working hands.

Seven Cups
of Water

MARY ANNE MOHANRAJ

MY BROTHER'S WEDDING DAY. THE FEASTING LASTED LONG PAST dark, and I went to bed exhausted. I first peeled off my sweat-soaked sari, rinsing my body with cool well water before changing into the white sari I wore to sleep. The old women had consulted the horoscopes of my brother and his young bride, had pronounced that this day, in this month, would be luckiest, in fact the only day that would not bring down a thousand curses on the young couple— never mind that it was also one of the hottest days of the year. There was no flesh left on the old women's bones, nothing that could drip sweat; I am sure they enjoyed making the young ones miserable.

I thought that, for once, I would be able to sleep. I'd been allowed a little of my father's whiskey, to celebrate Suneel's wedding; I had danced with the other unmarried girls. My sisters' friends giggled and preened as they danced, flashing their dark eyes and slim brown bellies at the young men who lounged by the door drinking. I just danced; I had no interest in catching a man. Not that any would have spared a glance for me, too-tall, dark Medha with coarse hair and a flat chest. I danced for myself, not for them. I danced until my feet were aching, until my arms and legs were lead weights. I danced until Suneel and his lovely Sushila were escorted to his bedroom, until the last piece of rich wedding cake was eaten, and the last guest had gone. Only then did I bathe and change, only then did I lie down on my bamboo mat, a few feet from my peacefully sleeping sisters. And still I could not sleep.

It might have been the heat. Our house is near the ocean, and usually cool breezes fill the small rooms, but that night it was so hot that it was hard to breathe. I kept thinking it would get cooler, but instead it got hotter and hotter. Sweat dripped in uncomfortable trickles from my neck to my throat, from my breasts to the hollow between them, pooling in my navel. My mouth was dry as dead leaves, and I finally rose to get some water.

The house was silent. I left my sisters sleeping, passed my parents' room, and my brother's. I passed the main room, where dying flowers and bits of colored foil testified to the day's happy event, and finally entered my mother's huge kitchen. We weren't rich, but we did have one of the largest houses in the village. We needed it; I was the youngest of eight, and cooking enough food for us all took many hands and pots in the kitchen. The moonlight streamed in the window, illuminating the rickety table where my mother chopped, the baskets of onions and garlic and ginger and chilies, the pitcher of water that was always kept filled. It was one of my mother's rules—if you drank from the pitcher, you refilled it from the well. With five daughters and three sons, she needed many rules to keep peace in the house. Not that we always obeyed them.

I stepped over to the pitcher, took a tin cup from the shelf, and poured myself a cupful. Then I saw her. Sushila huddled in the far corner of the kitchen, her back pressed flat against the baked mud walls, her red wedding sari pulled tight around her, so tight that the heavy silk seemed to cut into her fair skin. Folds of fabric were wrapped around her fists, and those in turn were pressed tight against her open mouth. She looked as if she were trying not to scream, but she didn't move or make a single sound.

I stepped toward her. "Sushila?" I knelt at her feet. Her knees were pulled up tight against her chest, and I rested a hand on one. "Are you all right?" It was a silly question, and after a moment I understood that I didn't deserve an answer. The cup was still in my other hand; at last I stretched it out to her. "Would you like a cup of water?"

She nodded and slowly lowered her fists. I raised the cup to her lips and tilted it so that she could drink. Sushila took a deep gulp, draining half the cup. Her whole body shivered then, though the water couldn't have been cooler than lukewarm after sitting all night. She shivered again and again, her arms now hanging loose at her sides, her eyes wide.

I didn't want to ask my next question, but I had to. "Did Suneel . . . did he hurt you?" The words almost choked in my throat. My second sister had married a brute who beat her; she came crying home every week to show us the bruises, and then turned right around and went back to him. I knew that there were men like that in the world; it was part of the reason I never wanted to marry. But Suneel—he had always been the gentlest of us all. He had converted to Buddhism a year ago, had turned vegetarian and mourned every time he accidentally stepped on an insect. He never teased me like the others had; he'd protected me from the worst of my oldest sister's rages. My favorite brother—I didn't want to believe that he could have hurt Sushila, but there she was, shaking before me . . .

Sushila shook her head. No. After a moment, the word came up and out of her throat—"No." I was almost as glad to hear the sound of the word as the sense of it; there was a crippled child who lived in the alley nearby who could not speak at all. I raised the cup again, and she drained it in another gulp. I put it down, not sure what to do next.

She was still shaking. I leaned forward, pulled her into my arms. When she was completely enclosed in my arms, the white of my sari covering the red of hers, she turned her head so that her mouth was against my ear. Her breath was hot against my neck as she whispered, "I'm bleeding . . ." Before I could speak, she reached up and took my right arm, her fingers sliding down to my hand, pulling it down under the sari to the space between her thighs. Her legs were wet, and when I brought my hand up, the tips of my fingers were stained red. When Sushila saw the blood, she started to cry.

I wrapped my arms around her and held her tightly, letting her cry against me. My second sister had shared every detail of her wedding night with us; she seemed to enjoy our shock and fascination. I knew that Sushila was the oldest daughter in her family, that her mother had died years ago of a fever. But didn't she have any aunts? I stroked her hair, so soft and fine, and told her softly, "It's all right . . . shhh . . ." Her shaking eased, slowly, though the tears still fell hot against my neck, sliding down my chest and mixing with my sweat, an indistinguishable mix of salty waters. I held her, and rubbed her smooth back, and whispered the words over and over until she understood.

I asked her at breakfast the next day if she had slept well. Everyone laughed, and Suneel's face reddened. He had inherited my mother's pale skin, and every emotion showed through. Sushila smiled demurely and assured me that she had. I was glad for her, but I hadn't slept at all.

I had drunk cup after cup of water after she'd left, then refilled the pitcher from the well. A breeze had finally picked up, and the ocean's salt air had filled the rooms, caressing my body stretched out on its mat—but still, I couldn't sleep. I kept remembering how she had felt, her small body huddled in my arms, remembering the sweet trembling, the softness of her cheek against mine. I had held my sisters and countless cousins, of course, but this had been different. And at breakfast and lunch and dinner, throughout the day, I watched Sushila. She was slender and fair, a perfect foil to tall Suneel, and she moved as if she were dancing. She was clever too, telling small jokes that made everyone laugh. If only I could look like her, talk like her . . . well. Might as well wish for Krishna to come down and carry me off.

That night I dozed for a few hours, but in the deepest hours I woke, sweaty and damp. I wanted some water. I got up and walked down the hall.

She was standing near the kitchen window, drenched in moonlight. "I thought you might be awake," she said, turning as I came in.

My tongue stumbled, but I managed to say, "I just woke up."

"Thank you for last night." She was blushing, but her voice was firm and clear. There was no sign of the trembling girl I'd held in my arms; Sushila held herself straight and poised. "You must think I'm very silly."

"You're welcome. I don't think you're silly." The moonlight shaded the planes of her face, the delicate curves; it was almost like looking at a statue. I could have stood there watching her for hours. "Shouldn't you be in bed . . . with your husband?" My brother.

"I was thirsty. I often get thirsty at night." She was wearing white; a thin gauze sari that barely covered her limbs. Sushila's small arms and legs made her look almost like a child, but I knew she was sixteen, nearly as old as me. "I came for some water, but I couldn't find a cup."

The cups were in plain sight; perhaps the shelf was a little high for her. I reached up, pulling down the same one I'd used the night before. It had a small notch in one side, and you had to drink carefully or you might scratch yourself. It was different from all the others, and my favorite. I lifted the pitcher and found that it was almost empty. Someone hadn't refilled it. I poured what water was left into the cup and held it out to her. As she stepped forward to take it from me, she stumbled, and her outstretched hand knocked against mine, spilling the water over both our hands, splashing onto the dirt floor.

"Sorry!" She seemed frightened for a moment, though it was only water.

"It's all right. But that was all the water." I could draw some more from the well, of course.

Sushila sighed. I could see her breasts move under the thin fabric of her blouse. "I'm really very thirsty." She lifted her dripping hand to her mouth then and started to lick the water from it. Her tongue was small too, and licked very delicately, with determination. She slowly licked away every drop as I watched.

"Still thirsty?" I asked. Sushila hesitated, then nodded. I could have drawn more water, but instead, I took a small step forward, bringing my wet hand up to her slowly opening mouth. She reached out a hand and gripped my wrist, surprisingly tight. She took the cup out of my hand and set it on the table. And then she brought my hand to her mouth and started to lick.

I started shivering then.

When she finished, having carefully licked first the back of my hand, then the palm, and then taken each finger into her mouth, she let go of my wrist. My arm dropped limply to my side. Sushila's eyes were wide and still, her head cocked to its side like a little startled bird. She bit her lip and said, "Thank you. That's much better."

I didn't know what to say. If I said the wrong thing, this night would be destroyed, might as well not have happened. I wanted to take her damp fingers in mine and lick them, but when I opened my mouth, these were the words that came out: "Suneel might miss you."

Sushila took a quick breath, then nodded. "Now that I've finished my cup of water, I'd better go back to bed." She turned away to step quickly and quietly down the hall. I heard her pushing aside the curtain that covered their doorway, and then it fell back into place behind her. I picked up the pitcher and went out to the well.

The third night I didn't even try to sleep. I had napped a little during the day, and my mother had called me a lazybones. It didn't matter. They were only staying a few more days, just three more days and then they were getting on a train, leaving the north, going down to the capital where Suneel had secured a government job. The tickets were bought; plans had been made. This night, and then three more—that was all.

After everyone else had gone to bed, I went to the kitchen and waited. I watched the moonlight travel across the room. I counted the cracks in the ceiling, and the lizards that lived in the cracks. I listened to the wind moving through the coconut palms, and when I couldn't sit still any longer I went outside and picked shoeflowers from the garden. Their soft crimson would look lovely in her hair. I arranged them in circles on the table, and in the center of the circle, I placed the filled tin cup. I was bent over them, straightening a crooked flower, when I heard her step behind me. I stood up straight but didn't turn around. Her arms slid around my waist, and Sushila rested her head against my back. She started to whisper: "It's dry in that room. It's so dry. My mouth and skin are dry. The air is like breathing chalk. The heat is outside and inside and burning. It hurts to breathe."

Did she know what she was doing to me? She must have known.

I said nothing, just listened, just felt her slim arms around my too-solid waist, the unbearable warmth of her against my sweating back. My blouse covered so little; her cheek lay against my naked skin, her belly was hot against my lower back.

"Medha," she whispered, "I'm thirsty."

I took the cup of water from the table and turned to face her, still enclosed in the circle of her arms, so that now her belly pressed against mine. I raised the cup to her lips, but Sushila shook her head, keeping her lips tightly closed until I lowered the cup, confused.

She smiled. "Aren't you thirsty?" she asked.

Oh. Of course I was. Desperately thirsty. My hands, curved around the cup, had turned to ice, but my mouth was burning. I raised the cup to my lips.

I filled my mouth with water, soaking the dry roof of my mouth, my parched tongue. Then she raised up on her toes and opened her mouth; I bent down, and placing my lips on hers, I gave her water to drink. Sushila took it from me, sucking the water deep down her throat. She swallowed, and I felt the motion in my own lips. Then she pulled back, and for a moment my chest tightened with fear . . . but she said only "More."

I fed her the water from my lips, making each mouthful smaller and smaller, each transfer taking longer and longer. Finally, the cup was empty and not just empty but dry. She released me then and stepped back. She said the words, formally, the ones I knew she was about to say.

"Thank you for the cup of water. I should return to my husband."

I nodded, and Sushila disappeared down the hall. Of course she had to return. This was impossible, so impossible that it wasn't even explicitly forbidden—but if I didn't think about it too hard, maybe it would be all right. Three more nights.

On the fourth night, as I poured her cup, I pointed out that the well was full of water. If we left the kitchen, if we went behind the house to where the well stood, shaded by a large banyan tree— there were many shadows near the well, and there was much water within it.

"I shouldn't be away that long," she said. "Just long enough for a cup of water."

I wanted to protest but didn't. If I did, she might decide she wasn't that thirsty after all; she might simply go back to Suneel. It would be so much safer that way.

I have always loved my sweet brother.

The fourth night she took the cup away from me. Sushila dipped her small finger into it, then traced a line along my arm. She bent down and licked up the water. Then it was a line from my throat to the top hook of my blouse, and her tongue dipped briefly beneath the line of fabric to chase a drop of water. Then she knelt to draw a circle on my belly, a spiral ending in my navel, where she lingered, sucking gently, then not so gently.

I tried to take the cup, to at least dip a finger in, but she pulled it back. Her eyes were laughing, though her voice was clear and firm.

"I'm sorry, but I'm really very thirsty tonight. I need to drink it all."

Sushila pulled me down to my knees and turned me to drip water along my back. She seemed especially fond of the back of my neck, and I brought my hand to my mouth to stifle the moans that I could not keep down. Thank the gods that my father snores so loudly. You can hear him from the kitchen, his snores regular as the ticking of his prized gold watch. If he found us like this . . .

Half a cup gone when she turned me back around, and she paused a moment, staring at me. Her eyes were large and wide and dark, her lips so full they seemed bruised, bitten. I leaned forward, my own mouth slightly open, hoping that she might choose to put her wet finger inside it, then follow it with her mouth, but instead she reached up and pulled down my sari, so that the sheer fabric fell to my waist, leaving my upper body dressed only in my blouse. The blouse fabric was thicker than the sari, but I felt naked. She smiled then, scooping up fully half the remaining water in her palm, and she drenched my left breast.

She put her mouth to the fabric, sucking the moisture from it, the water mixed with my own sweat. I raised my hand to my mouth again, teeth closing down on flesh. Sushila started with the underside of my small breast, and then circled up and around. Spirals again, circling closer and closer until finally her mouth closed on the center and I bit down hard on the web of skin between thumb and forefinger, breaking the skin, drawing bitter blood. She sucked harder and harder, pausing at times to lick or bite, sucking as if she meant to draw milk out of my breasts, enough milk to finally quench her thirst. Eventually, she gave up the attempt. She released my sore breast, lifted her mouth away, and smiled when she saw my bleeding hand. Her eyes danced, daring me to let her continue. I could stop this at any time. I could smother the fire and walk away.

What would she think of me if I backed away? I could guess, and could not bear the thought of it. If I backed away, she would only return to her husband. He would have her for the rest of his life. Her body would lie under his, and he would bend to taste her breast.

I nodded acquiescence. She poured the rest of the cup's water onto my right breast and lowered her head again.

Fifth night, and one more to go. When Sushila came into the kitchen, I opened my mouth to speak, but she laid a soft finger against my lips.

"You seem very thirsty," she said. "You should drink the water." She filled my tin cup, filled it to the brim, and then handed it carefully to me.

"I am thirsty," I answered. "I'm burning up." I waited, but she just smiled. The next move was entirely mine. I hadn't slept—I'd been thinking all day and all night of how to make Sushila burn. I needed to match her ingenuity, her ideas, to push the game forward. I needed her to understand that this was more than just a game. We couldn't stop here, or even slow down.

I put my hand on her shoulder and pushed down gently; she obediently sank to sit cross-legged on the floor. She seemed so patient; Sushila could wait forever, unmoved. I needed to move her. The words pulsed through me—*one more night, one more night*. I didn't have time to be patient. I needed her burning, the way I was, a burn that spread from her center to her heart and tongue and brain; a fever that kept her from thinking, from playing, from leaving. I pushed down again; her eyes widened, but she obediently lay down, stretching her legs out straight with her arms at her sides, her sari stark and white in the moonlight, against the dark dirt floor.

I touched her eyelids, and she closed them. I stood and picked up my mother's chopping knife, cold and heavy in my hand. I had always been clumsy; I had dropped it many times and had cut myself as I chopped. But tonight I would be careful.

I pulled over a basket and, lifting out a handful of chilies, began to chop, as quietly as I could. The wind whistled through the palm trees, and my father snored, but still . . . I chopped the chilies finely, minced them the way my mother could never get me to do when it was only for cooking. I minced them until they were oil and ground bits, almost paste. Then I scooped them into a tin bowl, my fingers covered in hot oil and slowly starting to burn.

I knelt beside Sushila and placed the bowl and cup by her still body. I pulled loose the sari fabric, pulled it down so that her upper body was only covered by her blouse, as mine had been the night before. Then I started to unhook her blouse.

I expected her to protest, but she said nothing, didn't move. I don't know what I would have done if she had tried to stop me; stopped, I suppose. But she didn't, so I unhooked each clasp. I peeled back the fabric, baring her breasts. They were ripe and perfect, large dark mangoes bursting with juice. I was so thirsty. I let down my sari and undid my own blouse, freeing my small breasts. If we were interrupted now, there could be no innocent excuse . . . and yet it wasn't enough. *One more night.* I smeared the chili paste in a weaving line, starting with her navel, curving up over her belly, looping and swirling until I reached her breasts, then circling in as she had done, circling to the centers.

Chilies don't burn at once on the skin. They take time. To Sushila it must have just felt like some slightly gritty jam. Perhaps she thought I planned to lick it off—but there was a whole cup of water to use up, and first I wanted her burning. When I finished drawing my patterns, I put down the bowl. I sat back on my heels, and waited.

Sushila felt it first on her belly, the slight, growing burn. She shifted a little, uncomfortably. I watched. Her eyes started to open, and I placed my clean hand over them. She kept her arms at her sides, but her body began to twist, to raise up from the floor, to arch. It was useless. Her belly was heated, her breasts. They were getting hotter and hotter. Soon it would be unbearable.

"Please . . ." The word broke from her lips. I took the tin cup. I started with her navel, started rinsing the chili paste away, caressing the skin with wet fingers, relieving the pain. But there wasn't very much water in the cup. I could only dilute the chili essence, soften the intensity, and by the time I reached her breasts, the water was more than half gone. And there just wasn't enough water left to do her nipples, their darkness crowned by fiery red paste. I let Sushila open her eyes then, raised the cup and showed her its emptiness.

There were tears in her eyes, but her arms stayed perfectly still at her sides. I smiled down at her.

"Do you want to go back to your husband now?" The water was gone.

"I'm burning, Medha. I'm burning up."

My heart thumped. I lay down beside her, moved my head to her breast and took the fire into my mouth. I have never been able to eat very hot food. I swirled the chili paste on my tongue; I savored the burning flavor of it, mixed with her sweat. My tongue had been stabbed by millions of tiny pins. I wanted to suffer for her.

I suckled at her right breast, feeling her body shifting against mine, hearing her whimpers. I was afraid we would be heard. I moved to the left breast, and her hand came up to tangle in my hair, to keep me there. Her leg slid between mine, and I began to suckle again, rocking our bodies together as I did. Her breath left her in a tiny sigh, and at the sound, my chest exploded.

I went to bed that night knowing that small traces of oil undoubtedly lingered on her body, that she lay beside Suneel still burning for me.

One more night.

* * *

They planned to leave the next morning. I had been thinking all day, and when she came to me that night, I was ready with my arguments.

I took her hands in mine, caressing her soft skin under my rough fingers. When she smiled, I spoke. "Come away with me."

"What?" Sushila tried to pull away, but I held on. Her eyes were suddenly wide and frightened, and I held her fingers as tightly as I could, trying to reassure her.

"Come away. Take the tickets; we can trade them for another day and then leave together. We can go to the city; I can find work." I was whispering, but I willed her to hear how much I meant what I was saying.

Her mouth twisted in a way I had never seen before. "Work? Doing what? What can we do?" Her voice was low as well, but scornful. "Should we end up washing someone's filthy clothes? Lose caste, lose family—lose the future?" She did pull away then, sharply.

I wrapped my arms around my body, trying to slow my thumping heart.

"*You* are my future!" I wanted to shout the words, and keeping them quiet was almost more than I could stand. "It doesn't matter what we do to survive. Nothing matters but that you come away with me. I'm burning, Sushila."

"You're being foolish." Her eyes were disgusted, and my chest hurt. "I can't leave Suneel—you have nothing and I have nothing. I have the jewelry your family gave me; would you have me sell that so that we can buy rice and lentils?"

"Yes!" I was passionate; I was convinced. "It's not fair that we should be separated. It's not right, Sushila!" I reached for her hand, but she pulled away. She walked to the window and stared out as she spoke. Her voice had grown so soft that I could barely hear her.

"It's not right to leave, Medha. The jewelry, even my saris, belong to him, not to me. I belong to him. Would you have me abandon Suneel, leave him alone and shamed, without wife or the hope of children? Does he deserve that? Is that fair? It's not right to leave him. I have to go with Suneel."

What had happened to my Sushila, who had burned for me last night? She sounded so calm, so cold.

"It doesn't matter what's right or wrong. What's *really* wrong is that you should leave with him, that you should leave me here alone." I didn't know if I was making any sense—I just knew that I was desperate to say something, anything, that would keep her. But she wasn't listening to me.

Sushila turned back to face me. "It won't work. I'm sorry." She sounded like the statue I had once thought her, as if she were built of stone.

"But I love you! I love you!" My heart was breaking. It had broken and she was crushing the pieces under her heel. "Don't you care for me at all?"

Sushila's voice gentled a little. "I do care for you. But if they found us, they'd drag us back in shame. They might do worse. I had a friend—her husband died and they said she'd poisoned him with bad cooking . . . they burned her. They burned her alive."

I sucked in my breath, shocked that she would think . . . "My family wouldn't . . ." She cut me off before I could finish.

"No, you're probably right. They probably wouldn't. But Medha, it won't work. You know it won't. My place is with Suneel. There's no place for us out there. Just here, in the kitchen, without words. Just for these six nights. Just you, and me, and the cupful of water." Her voice had turned soft, persuasive, but I would not be persuaded. I wanted to surrender to her, but there was no time for that now.

"The cup! Is that what matters to you? The cup is *nothing*, Sushila. The cup is just a game, it's *your* game. It doesn't matter. You just want to play your game and then go off, safe in the arms of your husband, leaving me here." Leaving me alone.

"Safe? You think I'm safe with Suneel?" Passion was finally in her voice—but not the kind I'd wanted.

"He'd never hurt you." I was sure of that, at least.

She closed her eyes, squeezed them tight for a long moment, then opened them again. "Oh no. He's sweet, and gentle, and kind. He will try to be a good husband to me, and I will try to be a good wife to him. We will have children, if the gods are kind." There was the pain I felt, there in her voice. But it wasn't for me. "And after ten or twenty or thirty years of that, I will have all the juices sucked out of me; I will be dry as dust. I will die of my thirst and blow away on the wind. And that's the way it is; that's the way it always is. You're the lucky one, Medha." Sushila meant it, I could hear it, but I didn't know why.

"Lucky?" I didn't understand her, didn't know her. Who was this woman with flat eyes, speaking of dust?

"At least you are still free for a little longer. Take what pleasure you can of it. That's all we can do, Medha. Take a little pleasure when we can."

Sushila fell silent, and I did too, still thinking that there must be some other argument, some persuasion I could offer. I didn't believe what she was saying—I couldn't believe that was all there was for us. But I thought for too long.

"Come," she said softly, "take up the cup." It waited, full, on the table. I knew that she was trying to save what she could; it was our last night, the very last. But I couldn't do it. I grabbed the cup, held it in my shaking hands.

I said, stuttering now, "I—I don't care about the cup!" and turned it over, spilling every drop of water to the floor. My voice had risen—too loud, dangerously loud, but I didn't care. I didn't know what she'd do, if she'd rage and shout, if she'd drag me to the ground. But Sushila just turned and walked away.

I let her go, let her walk down the hall and disappear into his room. I had lost her entirely, and lost our last night too. I had wasted a cup of water for nothing.

* * *

I slept like the dead that night. Perhaps I didn't want to face the morning, hoped that she would just slip away without my having to face her again. My mother shook me awake.

"What, are you sick too? Get up, Medha—I need your help. Sushila's sick and they can't leave today. I need you to take care of her today."

I dressed quickly. Not gone yet! Not leaving today! I rushed to Suneel's room to find him standing over his wife, his cheeks pulled in. Sushila's eyes were closed, and she did look pale.

"Medha, she's nauseated. She's been throwing up all morning. Stay with her, will you? I need to go change our tickets."

I nodded, and he bent to give her a kiss, then left the room. Once he'd gone, her eyes opened, and she motioned for me to bend down. I did, and she whispered in my ear, "I made myself throw up. I decided to give you one more chance." When I pulled back, Sushila was smiling, and I was too. Perhaps I looked too happy, because all too soon she was saying, "Just one more night. Suneel and I will leave tomorrow."

"But . . ." I had visions of persuading her, if only she would stay a few more nights, a week, two . . .

"No, Medha. It's too dangerous."

My eyes were stinging, but I knew she was right. Each night we'd gone further, each night we'd taken more risks. If we kept this up, we would be caught, and if she wouldn't leave with me . . . then it was this, or nothing. I finally nodded agreement. Just tonight.

I stayed with her through the day; we didn't touch. We could perhaps have held hands, or stolen a few kisses, but that would have been going outside the game, and the game had kept us safe so far.

It was an eternity until nightfall.

When I arrived in the kitchen, she was waiting. Something was different. The tin cup sat on the table, and the pitcher, but something else as well—a stone. It was my mother's sharpening stone that she used for her knives.

"Help me," she said. She picked up the cup and ran the stone along the jagged edge. I thought at first she was dulling the edge, making it safer—but after a few strokes, I realized she was making it sharper. Sushila handed it to me, and I stroked it to greater sharpness. We passed the two items back and forth, the cup and stone, sharpening the edge to match that of a blade . . . and still I didn't know why. It didn't matter, though. I trusted her. Finally, she put down the stone and called the cup done. Three quarters of the rim was still that of a cup, safe and dull. But one quarter had a sheen of sharpness to it, and it seemed more than just a cup.

"Pull up your sari," she said. I was startled, but obeyed, pulling it up past my ankle, my calf, my knee, until almost all of my thigh was visible—"Stop." I stopped, obediently, and watched her do the same with her sari. Her legs were so smooth and fragile; for a moment, I felt like a great, hairy cow. But the moment passed. We were past that now.

"Cut me." She pointed to her thigh, and, suddenly understanding, I took the cup in my hand. I reached out, pressed it against her soft flesh, bit my lip, and sliced down. A short, sharp cut, barely half the length of my palm. She had exhaled once, sharply, but made no other sound. She took the cup from my hand and, with a swift motion, made an identical cut in my thigh. The beads of blood welled bright, shining in the moonlight, and for a moment I was so dizzy I thought I would faint. But then I steadied, and when she leaned forward and pressed the cuts together, blending our blood, I held firm. She kissed me then, and the world spun around us.

"Pour the water," she said. I poured the water into the cup with my left hand, spilling some onto the table. It didn't matter. I poured until the cup was full. She took it and carefully sluiced some onto our joined legs, pulling away as she did. The bright blood ran down, mixing with the water, diluting.

"Don't pour it all!" I trusted her, but I couldn't keep the words from coming out. When the water was finished, so were we . . .

"I haven't. See?" She showed me the water left in the cup, barely a mouthful.

"Good." I looked at our legs, at the cuts that would turn into scars that we would carry forever. Forever! She wouldn't forget me, and I would never forget her. But we had a problem. "If we let the fabric go, the saris will be stained. People will wonder."

She nodded, smiling. "We'd better just take them off."

It was so risky; it was the last time.

We carefully removed our clothes, holding them away from the now trickling blood. We piled the fabric on the table and then, carefully, eased to the floor. My leg hurt, but as she bent her head to kiss me, the pain mingled with pleasure.

My hand found her breast, and hers wrapped around me. We lingered over our pleasure until the sky began to lighten, and then we shared the last mouthful of water. By the time the household wakened I was back in my room, embracing the ache in my leg, trying very hard to remember everything.

When she left, she reached up to my ear one last time. In full sight of everyone, she whispered, "It's for the best, Medha. You'll be married soon, and you must try to be happy. I will always care for you."

I didn't say anything out loud, but I knew that I would never marry, and I swore in my heart that I would never love anyone as I had loved her.

The scar faded into nothing within a year. I cried when the last trace of it disappeared.

Sushila . . .

ACKNOWLEDGMENTS

So many to thank . . .

As always, the EROS Workshop has provided a pool of talented writers and eager critiquers; their work and dedication have raised the standards for erotic fiction, and I am grateful. I owe an ongoing debt to my stalwart staff at Clean Sheets, who endured several months with a rather abstracted editor-in-chief, and to Brian Peters, the best managing editor a girl could ask for. My local writers' workshops, both Callihoo! and the University of Utah group, were invaluable in revising my own story; I must also acknowledge the feedback of my journal readers, who gave both critique and praise at crucial moments.

Many writers and editors in the field offered all kinds of support, including helping me to find the authors and stories in this volume. Especially helpful were Marianna Beck, Susie Bright, Jane Duvall, Susan Fry, Carol Queen, and staff members at *On Our Backs*, *Good Vibrations*, and *Cleis*.

Of course this book wouldn't have been possible without the intensive work put in by the good people at Melcher Media; it was a pleasure working with them all, most especially Duncan Bock and Andrea Hirsh. And my heartfelt thanks to Bob MeCoy of Crown for his support and faith in this project.

Finally, my thanks and love to Karina Roberts, Karen Meisner, Lisette Bross, David Horwich, Susan Shelangoskie, Jed Hartman, and, as always, Kevin Whyte. Editing assistance in last-minute crunches, late night and early morning phone conferences, friendly shoulders and endless support. I couldn't have done this without you.

Francesca Lia Block is the author of nine books, including the best-selling *Dangerous Angels*. "Mer" also appears in *Nymph*, her collection of erotic stories. She lives in Los Angeles.

Poppy Z. Brite is the author of four popular novels, *Lost Souls*, *Drawing Blood*, *Exquisite Corpse*, and *The Lazarus Heart*. Her work has appeared in many publications, including *Rage*, *Spin*, and The *Village Voice Literary Supplement*.

William R. Burkett, Jr. is the author of *Bloodsport* and *Bloodlines*, two recent novels in an ongoing series of adventure science fiction.

Daniel James Cabrillo has contributed to *Clean Sheets*.

Heather Corinna is the founder and editor of two acclaimed on-line journals, *Scarletletters* and *Scarleteen*. Her work has appeared in *The Adventure of Food*, *Clean Sheets*, *Maxi* magazine, and *Viscera*. Her story, "The Door Into One Moment; Eternal," published in *Baacchor* magazine in 1999, was nominated for the Pushcart Prize.

Louise Erdrich is the author of *Love Medicine*, *The Beet Queen*, *Tracks*, and *The Bingo Palace*. Her fiction has been honored by the National Book Critics Circle, and several of her short stories have been selected for O. Henry awards.

Tabitha Flyte is a British author living in London. She has spent much of her career working as an English teacher and journalist in Asia. Two of her erotic novels, *Tongue in Cheek* and *The Hottest Place*, will be published this year.

Kristine Hawes is currently one of the fiction editors for *Clean Sheets*. She has published poetry and prose across the United States and Canada, and short stories in *Batteries Not Included* and *Exhibitions*. She lives in the San Francisco Bay Area.

Michael Hemmingson recently co-edited *The Mammoth Book of Short Erotic Novels*. His other books include *The Naughty Yard*, *Minstrels*, and *Snuff Flique*. His new novel, *Affair*, will be released next year.

Diane Kepler has published short fiction and nonfiction in *Clean Sheets*.

Mary Maxwell's erotic fiction has been published in *Herotica 3* and *Herotica 4*. Her first novel, *Wild Angel*, is an action adventure tale about a young girl adopted by wolves in Gold Rush California. Mary Maxwell also appears as a character in